SUPERNATURAL
Dating Agency

Hate, Date, or Mate?

ANDIE M. LONG

CONTENTS

To my tribe.

You're weirder than the people I make up, and I love it!

Never change and thank you for everything xo

CHAPTER One

Kim

What was the wolf equivalent of the doghouse? Because I was in it.

My misdemeanors? Well, let's see...

Dating a wolf from an enemy pack - check.
Losing five werewolf shifter clients in one evening - check.
Pissing off your newly pregnant, mega hormonal boss - check, check, check.

I was sitting in Shelley's office right now while she glared at me. It was most off-putting. I couldn't even bribe her with a coffee and a chocolate doughnut because she'd started drinking blood, which she was decanting into a tomato juice bottle to fool other clients.

Shelley's arms were folded across her chest. "You have until the end of the week to get me five new clients."

I sighed.

"You lost us Darius, Sierra, and Jett. Plus two more of Darius' pack quit."

I pouted. "Sierra doesn't count. Darius only got her to join to make me jealous."

"She was still paying her fees."

I held a hand to my breastbone. "Can you stop thinking about your business for a moment? I'm in deep shit, Shel. Ebony says I'm going to cause a pack war. A. Pack. War. Also, I have to date Darius because of my binding deal with Lucy. How do I do that when he won't speak to me? Huh?" I shook out my right arm. "This stupid appendage keeps feeling like it's having its own menopause and Lucy says it will continue to feel occasionally like it's burning until he goes out with me. Jett won't answer my calls either. I need understanding, not more pressure. I don't deal with stress well."

Shelley snorted. She actually snorted at me. "If you don't have clients, you don't have a job do you? Now that's stress."

"Gaaahhhh."

"Oh for goodness' sake. You have five minutes to moan on, during which time I'll be your best friend. Then I'm back to being a boss and you have to bring in five more clients to replace the income you've lost."

"Supernatural ones?"

"Ideally, but I'll accept any at this time."

"Okay." I lowered my chin to my chest. *God, I have a great rack.*

Shelley looked at her clock. "Five minutes starting from now."

Fuck, I'd better get it all out quickly, like when you're trying to name everything you remembered on The Generation Game. "It's not fair, Shelley. I found the sexiest red chemise with a hooded robe. I was gonna go all Red Riding Hood on his arse."

"Whose? Jett's?"

"No! Are you even listening? I dated Jett to make Darius jealous."

"Um, you've been telling us all you didn't want to date Darius."

I slapped myself in the forehead. "So, I lied, okay? I've been having a crisis. I don't do relationships, and Ebony said I was destined for him. That's a relationship, right? Like a bloody long one. So I panicked. How come if a normal person panics they just might need to buy a bunch of flowers and say sorry, but I start a pack war? A Pack. War."

"So, what exactly is a pack war? It doesn't sound good in any case. Anything with the word war in it is a little worrying."

"You think? I don't know but I've started one. What if they all die? What if Darius now dies? Or Jett?" My traitorous mind imagines Sierra Forrester lying bloodied on the ground. *That's just so bitchy, Kim, and an evil thought too far. Why am I smiling? Stop it.*

"So what's the plan then? Just sit back and see what happens? I'm sure if there was any immediate danger to Withernsea I'd have been alerted."

A sip of my coffee was required. God, that was lush. "I've asked Frankie if he can send me a history of the shifters. Of both the packs, both here and at Hogsthorpe, and a potted history of shifters in general. The more information I have at my fingertips, the more I'll know what to do next."

"Well, I don't see that there is anything else you can do right now. Just keep trying to phone Darius to apologise and wait until your reading material comes through. And in the meantime, stay out of trouble and get me those clients."

I blew a huge breath out making a puh noise and then

sat up straighter and crossed my legs. "How are you anyway? Are you adjusting to life as an expectant mama?"

Shelley nodded. "To be honest, I wouldn't know I was pregnant if it wasn't for the O-neg I've started drinking. I have five months to go according to having a vampire baby, maybe even eight if it ends up being like a regular human/wyvern/witch baby. I'm quite chill about it all."

"Like a regular human/wyvern/witch? Have you heard yourself? Will it come out with fangs? Scales? A broomstick? What about red eyes? Are you having a home birth because how do you explain its potential peculiarities in the labour ward?"

A serious amount of eye rolling occurred. "It will come out like a regular baby: without teeth and with blue eyes. And there's Dr Fielding at the hospital, along with a whole host of other medical staff who know full well that Withernsea is full of supernaturals. Mine isn't the first supe baby to be born here."

"I still can't get over that. Even though we run a dating agency for them, so many people here are like the undead, or have real life talons. Must be a twat having a manicure if you're a bird shifter."

Shelley ran her hands through her hair. "Can you go to your office now? Time's up and you're wearing me out."

"Thanks a bunch."

As I stood up to leave, the door banged open and Lucy walked in clutching two coffees. She passed one to me, sat opposite Shelley, and put the other one in front of her on Shelley's desk.

"What's happening, dudes?"

"We are not dudes." I protested. "I hate people use that word for everyone. Makes me think I've grown a penis, and I didn't realise."

Lucy tilted her head towards me, then looked back at Shelley. "What's got into her today, or rather not got?" She cackled.

"Oh just because you're loved up." I did a mock vomiting impression. "Anyway, how come you're up at this time? Shouldn't you still be at it with loverboy?" Lucy was dating my ex, Frankie.

"He's sleeping. Vampire, remember?" She rolled her eyes. *Why was everyone rolling their eyes at me today?* "But for your information, I'm up keeping an eye on a client. The quicker I get my earth angel duties done, the quicker I can become an angelic housewife and just stay at home serving my man."

We both gawped at her.

"Oh my God, you didn't seriously believe that bollocks did you?" She guffawed.

"Are you supposed to blaspheme and swear when you're a helper of the angelic realm?" I creased my brows at her.

She wafted her hands as if wafting my words away. "I can't help blaspheming. After not being able to hear those words for twenty-odd years, I can't stop saying them all. Holy moly, oh my God, oh my fucking God, Christ almighty. It's so refreshing. Anyway, Angel Sophia told me that as long as I wasn't actually harming anyone I was fine."

"I'm not sure that's what she meant, Luce. I think she was referring to that one specific occurrence of a rude word you did right in front of her."

"Po-tay-to, po-tar-to,"

I stared at her, my hands on my hips. "Why was I expecting you to be all lovely now you are no longer a demon?"

"I'm a beginner earth angel; I don't think we're quite ready to move to the miracles stage yet."

"So who's this client then?"

She smiled brightly and rose an inch up off the floor, just hovered there and didn't even notice. "He's called Seth, and he's a new assistant in Jax's coffee shop, so I shall bring you regular coffees while I do my job."

"And what do you have to save him from?"

Lucy pulled a dramatic face. "Oh I'm not allowed to tell you that. It's a celestial secret. I can tell you one thing though. That man is hot. H.O.T. hot."

"How else would you spell it?"

"Kim! Your grumpiness and rudeness is out of order today. Go to your office, right now." Shelley glared at me again, and pointed at the door.

"Huh." I stomped out, taking my coffee with me.

It was seriously like I'd been sent to the naughty corner. I powered up my laptop. No new clients had applied. FFS. If we'd had five—or even better, more than five—new applications for membership, I could have got away with having to find any. I moved onto my own emails. I'd start work in half an hour when my coffees had had a chance to kick in.

There was an email from Frankie.

From: Frankielove@yahoo.com
To: Kim@withernseadating.com
Date: Wed 25 Jan 2018 Time: 10:02 am
Subject: General shifter information

Hey Kim.
While I dig a little deeper into the specifics,

here are some factoids about the shifters in general. Document attached.
From your mate (get it? Lol)
Frankie

I clicked on the attachment and opened the document, saving it to a brand new folder I named 'get self out of the shit'. Then I sat back and read it.

GENERAL WOLF SHIFTER INFORMATION

(Not to be reproduced. Copyright F. Love, 2018)

Werewolf (werwulf, man-wolf, lycanthrope)

The ability to shift into a wolf from human form.

The rumour that you can become a werewolf from a scratch is untrue folklore. In reality you have to either be born a were, or in the instance of a mate, bitten during the mating ritual under a full moon.
Weres are vulnerable to silver and can be killed by being shot by a silver bullet to the heart.

Weres can shift at any night through choice, but on the night of a full moon will always change. This is when mating rituals occur. It is not true that wolves rampage at this time with a lack of control over their animal selves.

Mates primarily come through the pack; however due to a lack of female offspring (8 out of 10 were births result in

male children), mates are often selected from out of the pack.
Weres mate for life.

A male werewolf is expected to take a mate no later than at
the age of thirty years and can be ostracised from the pack if
still single by then.

I clicked into Darius' profile. He'd recently had his 29th birthday. That was a plus for me. I could just wait it out until he got desperate. Although what if he was already desperate and so mated with Sierra? Yes they were friends, but we all knew it was nigh on impossible for males and females to really be friends. Did that mean he might have shagged her before?

He will have slept with people Kim. You're no saint yourself, remember?

I rang his mobile phone. Once again it went to his answering service.

"I'm not able to take your call right now and if you are Kim, quit ringing. I told you we're done."

Rude.

We're done. Were done. Hahahahaha. He'd said a joke without realising.

Not to be thwarted from my current mission, I sent a text.

Kim: I really am very, very, sorry. BTW your voicemail is rude and unnecessary.

My phone soon beeped with an incoming message alert.

Darius: Stop texting.

Kim: I will if you'll meet me to talk.
Darius: I have nothing further to say to you. You
brought shame on me.
Kim: Give me a chance to make amends,
pleeeaaassseee. Pretty please with cherries
on top?

This message failed to send <<communication error>>
Had he blocked me?

My bloody arm set off with another hot flush. "Ah, Hell, it's not my fault he won't date me." I yelled in the direction of the floor. Then I realised it was my fault, so I sat and sulked for a minute.

Then I tried to ring Jett.

"I'm not able to take your call right..."

"For crying out LOUD." I ended the call and threw my phone on the desk in temper. Thank God it had a protective case. Well, there was nothing else to do, so I should just get on with my work, which included finding five new customers. I stood up, grabbing my jacket and handbag. I'd go to Jax's coffee shop. Not only could I look for potential new clients and get some lovely coffee but I could have a nosy at this sex god, Seth. It would take my mind off other things.

∼

Whoa!

The queue to the front of the coffee shop counter extended out of the main door. No way was I waiting in that. Jax was my friend. I passed a load of women in the queue and then as I got halfway I stopped—stunned.

9

In front of me was a blonde haired guy in jeans and a white tee wearing a barista apron that said 'Jax's' on it. What played in my head was a fantasy movie-reel of him in a shower, the spray bouncing off a hard ripped man chest, while he bit his lip and looked at me with a lusty wink.

"Kim!" Jax shouted. "Come meet the new guy, Seth. He's proving a hit. We've never been so busy."

Much to the consternation of the rest of the queue, I stalked right to the front making sure my skinny-jeaned ass sashayed as I did so. I held out a hand. "Hey, Seth. I'm Kim. I work at Withernsea dating just upstairs and along."

He gripped my hand. Hmmm, firm handshake, smooth warm skin. Clean fingernails. All good signs.

"So what can I get you? I guess as a regular I'd better make sure to remember your order."

A bed and your cock please.

"A latte and a chocolate doughnut please."

Down, girl.

"Coming right up." He beamed a huge smile at me. Oh God he had cheek dimples. I was going to be a puddle on the floor in a minute.

When he served me my coffee, I leaned closer. "So, Seth. Sorry to be so direct with this but I'm looking at this queue. Do you have a girlfriend?"

"No. I got divorced recently. My ex cheated on me." He shrugged.

"Do you fancy joining the books?" I asked him. "Say, one month's free trial?"

"Sure, why not? Drop me a form in." He said.

I went into my purse where I always carried a few copies. "Can you get it back to me by five?"

"Okay." He served me my order and a side of another beaming smile.

As I walked back up the queue, I stopped to talk to the other women waiting. "Hey, I'm Kim from Withernsea dating. We just signed Seth onto our books and we have several other men just like him if any of you are interested in signing up."

I walked out with twelve new applications and some of them had ticked the 'extra supelemental information' box (it looked like a typo to humans but actually wasn't) the dating agencies code for supes. I'd eaten my doughnut and drunk my coffee while women filled out the application, so I walked back to the office and knocked on Shelley's door.

"Come in."

Her face flashed with annoyance as I walked towards her.

"Where have you been? You'd think given our conversation this morning that you might have actually stayed at your desk and worked."

I placed the application forms on the table. "Twelve new customers, and a 'lucky' thirteenth shall be here and on your desk by five-thirty." I high-fived myself. "You were saying?"

Shelley grinned. "I was saying what an asset to my company you are, Kim. Thank you. Enjoy the rest of your day."

I felt good, so I sashayed out of Shelley's office too.

Now there was just those pesky wolves to deal with.

CHAPTER
Two

Darius

"How long are you going to be wearing that face?" My younger sister Alyssa asked.

"I'm not wearing a 'face'." I protested.

She tilted her head to one side. "You look like someone tea-bagged you with a sweaty bollock."

"Alyssa Dakota Wild, you'll have your mouth washed out with soap if I hear you say that again."

"Sorry, Mum." She said, while simultaneously rolling her eyes at me.

Fifteen-year-old sisters were a challenge. I couldn't imagine trying to parent her.

"Look at him though, Mum. He's been like it for days now."

My mum came over and sat beside me on the couch.

"It's true you're not yourself, Son. I know you were disappointed about the woman, but she still might be the one. We have to wait now."

"I really liked her, Mum. But what she did, dating Jett. I'm not sure I can forgive that. I don't understand why she'd date him and not me."

"She's asked to meet you. Why don't you go and see if she can explain? It's better than sitting looking constipated." Alyssa sniped.

13

"How do you know she's asked to meet me? Oh my God, have you read my messages again?"

"Well, you do leave your phone hanging around."

I stood up and got right in Alyssa's face, I saw the yellow flash of my wolf eyes reflected in the shades she was now wearing. She thought they looked cool. It wasn't even sunny, and we were indoors.

"Keep out of my stuff and my business, or I'll borrow your DKNY sunnies and accidentally sit on them."

"Darius, sit back down. It's not your sister's fault things have been a little rough for you lately."

Alyssa moved her glasses up to the top of her head so I could take in her smug smile.

"Alyssa. The dishes need taking out of the dishwasher. Go make yourself useful."

She huffed and left the room.

My mum stared at me a moment and then began speaking. "So, I went to see Ebony today."

I scrubbed a hand through my hair. "Mum, why did you do that?"

"Honestly? Your dad had pissed me off, and I decided to go have a good spend, and her boutique is the best in Withernsea. But as soon as I got in there she started with the visions. I actually felt sorry for her. They give her terrible migraines."

"She got the vodka out then?"

"Yes and I had one, so she didn't look odd. Poor woman, it's the only thing that helps her."

I clasped my hands tightly, my knuckles whitening. "Go on then, you know you're dying to tell me what she said."

"Darius. I'm not dying to tell you. You're my oldest son and I'm looking out for you, that's all."

I sighed. I really was a grumpy bastard of late. "Sorry, I know. I'm just frustrated with all this mating stuff."

Now I was in my thirtieth year the pressure had ramped up. I'd wasted months trying to pursue Kim Fletcher, the super-hot woman at the dating agency who handled the organisation of dates for our kind. My mind floated back to when I'd first properly met her...

I'd seen her before, around Withernsea. Her long dark hair framing a heart-shaped face. But it was her smell that appealed the most. She smelled to me like the finest scotch, mixed with sex. She smelled like she was mine. I'd been called to the agency after there'd been a fire bomb aimed at Shelley's office. I'd made sure my cop uniform was on point, my police shirt tight against my pecs and my slacks hugging my arse. One thing all the running around in the woods did was give you a great ass and thighs. I knew I looked like a walking Magic Mike stripper.

As soon as I'd walked past her, she'd yelled "Holy fuck," before covering her mouth and pretending to have the hiccups. I'd tried not to smile at her reaction, which wasn't all that difficult because when I met her gaze something strange happened. It was like we were locked in a staring competition. I couldn't take my eyes off her.

It took for Shelley to remind me I'd come to view a crime scene before I'd been able to break away.

When I'd returned to Kim's office I started staring at her again. There was something in me, like an invisible thread that was dragging me to her, and that smell... I just wanted to leap over the desk and bury my nose in her neck and nuzzle her.

I'd needed to leave but didn't want to. What could I say to get her attention? I decided to remind Shelley about my application hoping Kim would take the hint and date me herself.

"Just to say that I sent in an application for the agency. I'm young, free and single. Well, I'm not free on a full moon, but the rest of the time."

But Kim only nodded her head before her gaze had returned to her computer screen.

She'd been in a casual relationship with a magician called Frankie before Satan had smote him and he'd ended up turned into a vampire. Since then I wasn't aware that she'd dated anybody. I'd thought I was in with a chance, but then she'd arranged dates for me with other women, and herself flirted with other men.

When I'd seen her in a restaurant with Jett Conall, one of our enemy pack, a few days ago, it had been the last straw. If she knew what she had started I'd never be able to forgive her, and that's why I'd been putting off seeing her.

"Earth calling, Darius." My mum nudged my shoulder.

I turned to her. "I'm listening."

"So Ebony says Kim's actions will set in train a challenge between you and Jett for Kim's heart, but there is also a shadow hanging around, a third suitor. She foresees not only a challenge for Kim, but also one to our pack as the wolves of Hogsthorpe will be able to challenge Withernsea for power if Jett mates with a Withernsea resident."

"So how come they haven't already made such a challenge? There are plenty of single women in Withernsea."

"The rules are that they can't seek a date, but in this

case Kim asked him. She looked him up on the computer. They were finding a loophole anyway. Applying to the agency was a way of meeting a woman. If he'd gone out on an arranged meet and convinced his date to ask for a second date that would have done it. It was only a matter of time. The wolves are bored in Hogsthorpe—restless. Ebony says she can hear their inner wolves howling with confliction."

"So Kim did this, but the chances were it would have happened anyway?"

"Yes, Son."

"And not only is Jett my enemy but there could be another man?"

Surely it couldn't be Frankie? He was loved up with Lucy now.

"That's what she said. Now you need to have a really clear think on whether or not you're going to pursue Kim. If she is the one for you, I will help you all the way, Darius. But it will not be easy. We must speak to Alpha Edon and listen very carefully for his directions. This is very much pack business, Darius, even though it's your mating and your heart."

I sighed. "I know. Why does it have to be so complicated though?"

My mum stroked my hair. "Because it's love, Son; and love is complicated, but worth its challenges."

She left me, going to the kitchen. We lived in a large wooden cabin built in the woods at the edge of Withernsea. No residents here knew it existed as we'd surrounded the land in front of the woods with a caravan park and had got a wizard to erect a glamour which meant that anyone staying in the park only saw farmers fields when they looked out of their window. A perimeter fence with security warnings stopped anyone venturing any further than the caravan park boundary. Some of the pack had chosen to live in the caravans, preferring that to a wooden structure. I would have the choice once mated to build a home in the woods or accept a brand new caravan or lodge. I would let my mate choose our home. All I would be interested in was making sure she was happy and satisfied.

I decided I would speak to Alpha Edon before I made any further decisions about Kim as my possible future mate. I'd need to be sure to accept my responsibilities as a member of the pack and put that before love. The safety of my pack was paramount.

"So have your balls dropped yet? Are you going to get your woman? Or do you want to borrow a tampon?"

Alyssa was back.

Yes, safety was paramount, even that of annoying little sisters.

CHAPTER

Three

Kim

"You do know I had your boyfriend resident in my office for months, don't you? I just got rid of him and now you're hanging around. What gives?"

Lucy looked up from her eReader. "I'd gotten to a really interesting bit then. Can't you just get on with your work? Seriously, you spend a lot of time distracted from your duties, you really do. I mean twenty-three-and-a-half minutes looking between Darius, Jett, and Seth's profiles. I suppose that's due to your selfless dedication to find them dates, even though two of them aren't even on your books anymore and you used the other for recruiting purposes."

I narrowed my eyes at her.

She placed the eReader on her lap. "It's a good job Satan regenerated because the old one would have really seen your potential." She flicked back her fringe. "Anyway, in answer to your question, I need to be around here for my whole earth angel post. I have to keep an eye on Seth, and also an eye on Shelley to make sure that her baby is safe, but don't you be telling her I'm doing that."

I dropped my pen in shock. "Is her baby in danger?"

"Not at the moment as news hasn't got out yet. She's yet to announce it beyond close family, right? But her and Theo, and her parents, are very aware that this child is prophesied as the ultimate leader of Withernsea. The most powerful supernatural ever. There are going to be a few folks not so happy with that idea."

"I never thought. Poor Shelley. It's bad enough dealing with morning sickness when you're drinking blood—seriously, it's like the exorcist or something—but to have people want to harm you and your baby? That just doesn't bear thinking about."

"Which is why she has an earth angel hanging around. So, if it's okay I need to stay around here a while. Well, between here and the coffee shop. If there was a spare unit I'd look at renting a space because I'm putting together Frankie's encyclopaedia of all the supernatural species while I'm between angel duties. I'm just reading through the first chapter now." She picked up the eReader and shook it at me. "He's in his element putting this together and learning so much about all the different kinds of supernatural beings."

"Just stay there a moment. I need to have a word with Shelley about something. I'll be right back."

"I've no intention of going anywhere but it's kind of you to make the gesture." Lucy picked the eReader back up. "I'll be leaving at 4pm when Frankie is due up though, because he's due *up* if you catch my drift and I'm going to oblige him."

I shuddered at the thought. Lunch could wait. It was even worse given that he was my ex because my mental image of him with Lucy was a little too vivid given our past. I knew she was guaranteed a good time and didn't blame the woman for going home promptly. But still, I didn't need to know he was an alarm cock so to speak.

I wandered through to Shelley's office. "Hey, you got a minute?"

"Ooh sounds serious. Sure, sit down."

"Lucy's here again. She has earth angel shit to do and needs to be around. Do you think if I got the staff room emptied of the junk in it, she could go in there? We don't use it and she has the money to pay a monthly rental. Also, she has spare time when she's not earth angeling. She's got managers in at Red's now because she wants to spend her evenings concentrating on Frankie's meat and two veg instead of any at the steakhouse. I was thinking she could learn the ropes and cover your maternity leave?"

Shelley raised her eyebrows and shot me a questioning gaze. "Do you think she'd be up for that?"

"I don't know. I thought I'd sound you out first, but she's typing up Frankie's manuscript which means she's learning all about supernaturals. God, what if she ends up better at my job than I am? Please don't sack me when she's awesome!"

"She might end up awesome at knowing things, but as an employee I think she'd be even harder to control than you are. Can you see me setting her regular hours? She got damn selfish spending all those years in Hell. She's getting better now she's with Frankie and has lost the demon horns, but she's a way to go with developing her good side. I mean she set my office on fire last year."

"Yeah but that's when she was evil and she can't flick fire out of her fingers anymore."

"Oh yeah? Have you checked her handbag? She's started carrying lighters... and she doesn't smoke."

"Do you think Angel Sophia was having a mental break-down when she gave Lucy this job?"

"I trust our celestial beings know what they are doing. I have enough to think about down here, never mind up there."

"Of course. How's your training going?"

"My father feels we need to meet more regularly now with the baby coming. Now Satan has been replaced by a new version it means that other supernaturals are likely to descend on Withernsea, not believing I am a worthy opponent while pregnant. They'll try to use my pregnancy to their advantage in gaining control. It might be worth keeping an eye out for any strange applications to the dating agency as gaining an interview here would give them direct access to me."

"That's true. Listen, if Lucy comes on board, we will vet all the new applications and do all the interviews. You can focus on the rest of the work."

"Appreciated. Being pregnant with a vampire's baby is hard enough without all the stress of the ruler of Withernsea crap."

"And how is the Daddy-to-be?"

"Smothering. Thank goodness he has to sleep during the day and also that he doesn't need to breathe, or I might be smothering him too—with a pillow."

I laughed. "Right, I'm going to go back and see if Withernsea dating is recruiting a new employee. Can we afford it?"

"Sure, I have a rich vampire husband anyway to fall back on if things get tight while I have the baby."

"I think things are likely to get loose." I quipped.

"Yeah well, I'll be doing Kegels daily don't you worry about that. I've got to keep my vampire lover happy for many, many years. Hey actually that's another point in the favour of being turned before the birth. I'd keep my tight vajayjay."

"I thought you weren't interested in being turned? That you wanted to wait until after the birth?"

Shelley fiddled with a paperclip on her desk. "I've been speaking to the medics at the Caves and there's no risk to the baby. In fact I'd probably be a healthier mum if I was turned. It's just the whole feeling like I have the flu, dying, agonising thirst thing that's putting me off."

"I don't know why, that was your every Friday and Saturday night pre-Theo."

"Ha-ha."

~

"Lucy? I have a proposition for you."

The eReader went onto her lap again and she sighed. "I knew this would happen. That you wouldn't be able to accept me and Frankie together. I'm sorry but I don't swing that way, I already told Maisie this. So no. No threesomes."

"Eww." I actually did gag. "That's not it."

"God, you are so dramatic. If I did swing that way you'd be thoroughly satisfied and begging for more, so drop the norovirus look."

I shook my head as if I could dislodge her thoughts from my mind. "God, I'm starting to regret my looking out for you now." I told her. "Now get up and come follow me."

She sighed but stood and followed me out of the room and across the small landing. I pushed open the door to our staff room. It was a small room with a table and four chairs, sink, kettle, cupboards, and boxes full of crap that needed sorting out—mostly electronic equipment that had broken and it had been easier to just dump it. We'd not used the staff room as we had Jax's below. Jax's coffee and doughnuts were legendary.

"What is it you're showing me? The world record for

dust bunnies? There's a whole fucking warren in here. You need pest control." She sneezed.

"This potentially is your new office. We could work through the boxes together. I'm sure between you and Shelley you could come up with a redecorating budget. Jax's brother would do a good deal on it. It would give you an office of your own and also, if you want it, there's a job to go with it."

"I'm not going to be your cleaner. Just because you're a filthy whore."

"I'm sure your ex could vouch for that fact but no that's not it, you ungrateful cow. Now shut it and listen up before I change my mind and just lock you in here."

"Fine."

"You're here all day, and your earth angel duties are intermittent, right?"

"Correct."

"So you're helping Frankie put his guide together..."

"Also correct."

"Shelley needs someone to cover her maternity leave so our proposition is why don't you work for us freelance? You can use the office and juggle Frankie's guide, earth angel duties, and working for the agency. You'd be helping me interview potential new clients. Plus, with you working on the guide, it would be fantastic to have your expertise on all the supes. You're bound to learn all about them as you put the guide together."

"I would have to ask Frankie if I could share his work with you, given that he is going to make a living from this masterpiece."

"How much will his guide be?"

"Four dollars ninety-nine a month to access his database. A complete bargain."

"Then sign me up as an early-adopter."

She squealed and clapped. It was more scary than anything she'd ever shown me as a demon. "His first client. He'll be so pleased."

"So what do you think? Do you want to rent this room and work for the agency?"

"Yes. That would be fantastic. Would you be okay if I set up CCTV in here? I want to be able to keep an eye on Shelley and on the coffee shop."

"Is this legal?"

"Not in the slightest."

"I never heard you ask. Keep it in a lockable cupboard and if you ever grass on me I will paint your office red, turn the heat up full blast and be such a damn cow to you, you'd think you were back in Hell."

"You are so mean to me sometimes. I heartily accept all proposals. I shall go and get us coffees to celebrate and thus do a little earth-angeling at the same time while I check what Seth is doing."

As she walked past me she knocked a cobweb off my skirt. "I hope that's from the room and not your vagina."

The door swung shut behind her and closed before my mouth did.

CHAPTER

Four

Darius

I headed to an area at the edge of the woods where the community hall stood. This was where we held our pack meetings and ceremonies. We weren't a huge pack, with around thirty adult males, twenty-five adult females and then the kids. Altogether our group totalled around seventy. We had different duties around the park. I did some security detail alongside my job as a Police Officer.

Our Alpha, Edon, was around sixty years old and had been the Alpha male for the last twenty-nine years. Alpha's were elected by the rest of the adults in the pack. Edon was a charismatic leader with a huge presence. With short salt and pepper hair and a long grey beard, he stood for no nonsense. He was like an uncle to me. The whole pack were family to each other whether through blood or circumstance.

Any adults could attend the pack meetings but it was mainly the adult males who attended, following meetings with a game of pool, and a beer or scotch.

I walked into the meeting room looking at who was here already. There was Edon; his sons, Reid and Sonny; my stepfather, Billy; my younger brother, Rhett, who was twenty; and about another eight of the pack males. Alyssa had assured me that she would kick sexist butt when she was eighteen and could attend the meetings. I gave her two meetings maximum before she was bored out of her brain and back to taking selfies on Instagram. No one willingly wanted to attend, it's just how it was. Back in the old days tradition deemed it the man's role, and because it was boring, the women still let us get on with it. Some things were worth fighting about in equality, pack meetings weren't one of them. Everyone got a say in pack business anyway. My stepdad always warned me that when a woman put their mind to something not even being a scary arse wolf would stop them. "Your mum goes feral without changing if I'm not careful."

I took a seat around the large meeting table and poured myself a scotch.

Edon cleared his throat. "Okay, all, if you're ready. I'd like to get down to business."

We nodded and murmured our agreement.

"Right, the first thing on the agenda is I would like to announce the engagement of my eldest son, Reid, to Sierra. Their mating ceremony will take place in three full moon's time with their civil ceremony here in the hall. Invitations to come.

We all clapped and patted Reid on the back. He and Sierra had been together a long time. He was a good friend and Sierra had been my best friend for years. She was a year younger than me, so three years older than her fiancé. The pack had always thought Sierra and I would get together but we'd never felt that way about each other. As soon as Reid hit twenty-five the mating call had passed between them. I was so pleased for them both.

However, at the same time I felt a pang that Reid at twenty-five would be mated before me. It might have been my imagination, but I was sure I'd felt some of the others looking at me when Edon made the announcement. In one years time I'd be an embarrassment to the pack if I remained single.

Edon went through some other more mundane business before tapping his papers on the desk and then placing them down.

"Okay, the final discussion of the evening relates to the future of the Withernsea pack. Now I know there have been rumours going around. That ends right now. I'm going to tell you the truth and you make sure this gets back to those who need to know."

There were murmurs of agreement in the room.

"Darius was fated to mate to a human female, by the name of Kimberly Fletcher. However, things have gone awry and Kim ended up contacting Jett Conall and asking him on a date."

More murmurs along with surprised gasps circulated.

"So, that means at some point soon she will be forced to choose between them."

"Shame it's not the olden days when you'd just go in and bloody carry her out. Tell her to be quiet, she was yours and that's that." Said Bryan, our oldest member, at eighty-six.

"Yes, well times have moved on and you'd be arrested if you did that now."

"Can't arrest himself, can he? Can't he have a word with the bosses? Just go into that agency and get her, lad. Tell her who's boss."

"If I may carry on..." Edon gave Bryan a cool-eyed gaze and Bryan sat back suitably chastised. "The woman will have to choose and being a modern day woman could accept neither of the wolves and someone else entirely, a possibility given she has an entire database of available males at her disposal."

"So does Darius have to court her?"

"No. The Seer says that the woman has to do her own choosing. If she requests his company, Darius can attend but he can't tell her that the pack are under threat should she choose Jett."

"And if she doesn't want either myself or Jett?" I asked.

"Then they can't come back to Withernsea. Unless they find another female. The other option is we take them on in a pack challenge and run them out of the area altogether but that would be a last resort."

"So what's the plan of action?" I asked.

"If she asks to see you, you go. If she wants to speak to you, you speak. If she wants you in her bed you make sure you fuck her until she wants to scream no one's name but your own."

I guessed I needed to unblock her telephone number then.

"And what if she dates the other wolf as well?" I needed to clarify the arrangements.

"You can't interfere. Not until one of you mates with her. Once she agrees to be your mate, she is in effect engaged to you and will have to make a date for the mating and civil ceremony. We wish you luck, son." Edon said.

Everyone raised their glass. I drank several. The challenge was on and I knew that if I didn't win I might be out of the pack soon and more catastrophically we were all potentially out of Withernsea.

Back in my room, I unblocked Kim's number and waited.

There was nothing. It looked like I'd succeeded in driving her away. I called Sierra.

"Congrats, lady. I'd better be going to be the best man."

"Of course you are, silly. Thank you. Now how are you doing? Reid's just filling me in."

I'd bet he was. Newly engaged males were randy as all hell.

"I need a favour. Could I buy you a coffee tomorrow and one of the nicest doughnuts around?"

"Oooh Jax's?"

"Yeah."

"Okay. What time do you want to meet?"

"Well, that's the thing. I want you to go without me."

"Huh?"

"Let me explain."

~

The following morning just after 10am my mobile phone pinged.

Kim: *I demand you meet with me so I can explain everything. Stop being an arse Darius Wild.*

I sat back and laughed, waited five minutes and then sent a reply.

Darius: Fine. Where then? This better be good. I don't like my time being wasted.

In seconds I had a reply.

Kim: Eight pm. Hanif's. I'll pay.

Fuck. It went against every bone in my body to let a woman pay for dinner. I thought about my sister's face if I said this, growled, and typed my response.

Darius: See you then.

I opened up a new message to Sierra.

Darius: Thank you so much. You're a star!

Sierra: My pleasure. Her face was a picture. She deffo likes you, so something else must be holding her back. Anyway, good luck, bestie.

Hmm, could that be true? Was there something stopping Kim from being mine? I guess I needed to find out.

CHAPTER

Five

Kim

I'd spent the night catching up on *Stranger Things* on the television. I'd had a good nights sleep. Life was good.

Today me and Lucy were going to get the staff room cleaned up, so I'd tied my hair up in a ponytail and put on my painting clothes. No point in getting dressed up if we were going to be knee deep in dirt. Shelley would man the phones and keep an eye on the emails. All I needed to do was go get a coffee and doughnut from Seth to get a head start on the day. The eye candy wouldn't go amiss before all I could see was dust.

Once again the coffee shop was bustling. Jax spotted me and motioned for me to take a seat. Even better. Table service. She wandered over.

"The usual, babes?"

"Yes, please. Wow, it's not letting up in here is it? Are you this busy all the time?"

"This is slow. I don't know what Seth has but I need to bottle it if he leaves."

I laughed. "If only you knew before that the way to a successful coffee shop was a hot barista. Now the other women, and some men, of Withernsea will be getting hooked on your superior brand of coffee. They are so lucky."

"They are. Well, I'll be back in a moment with your order. You staying in or taking it back to the office?"

"Staying thanks. I don't start for another twenty minutes today."

"Do you know, I'm going to come join you. I could use a rest, it's been relentless."

I was pleased for Jax. She'd been running the coffee shop for three years now and it really was an amazing venue. Choose what had brought in the extra custom—her products reputation or the hot new assistant—she deserved every success. I looked around the space. The atmosphere was amazing with everyone laughing and chatting.

Then I saw *her*.

Seated at a table near the counter.

I'd been so distracted from looking at Seth, I'd failed to see the other person under my nose.

Sierra Forrester.

There she sat with a friend. The large beaming smile on her face revealed her white movie star style teeth. Her chestnut curls bounced as her head went back with laughter. Even her freckles seemed to dance across her nose and cheeks.

Bitch.

Then her friend grabbed Sierra's hand. Her left hand, and they both stared and admired a ring on her finger. My eyes zeroed in on it. At a large oval diamond. I checked out which finger it was on and felt my heart plummet. No. He wouldn't do that. Would he? Had Darius proposed to Sierra? What had I done?

I only realised I was staring rather rudely when Sierra's gaze caught my own.

Fuck, she was coming over! I froze.

"Hey there. Kim isn't it?"

"Yes, that's right." *Look at her, smile. Come on body do something!*

"The coffee here is fabulous. I shall have to come here more often although I'm not sure my fiance will approve of me hanging here with that hottie behind the counter. Am I right?"

"The coffee really is lovely here." I forced out, refusing to acknowledge her use of the word fiance lest I leap up and pull a few of her curls out.

She swept a few said curls out of her face, using the aforementioned hand. The dazzle almost blinded me as the sun hit the diamond.

Just then Jax arrived with my order and a drink of her own. She sat down. "Am I missing anything then?" She asked me. "Any gossip. News? I get so bored sometimes stuck behind that counter all day. We've not had a girls night out for ages, we must have one soon."

"No, nothing of any excitement to report." I said.

"I got engaged!" Sierra squealed. "Sorry. I know Kim. My name's Sierra." She held out her hand for Jax to shake. "Your coffee is delightful by the way. I shall tell all of my friends and the pack. I know Darius comes here a lot already. Now I know why he was always hanging around. I couldn't understand why he was always here before. Now I know. It's the coffee and doughnuts."

And me you cow. Before you stole him.

"Is that who you're engaged to? Darius Wild?" Jax looked shocked as well she might.

Sierra giggled for longer than she needed to. *Yeah rub it in, cow. You won. I was an idiot.*

"Oh God, no. Ewww. Darius is my best friend. He's like a brother to me. No, I'm engaged to Reid Woodland."

"Oh I don't think I know him. You'll have to bring him

in and have a coffee and bun on the house from me in celebration." Jax said. "Won't she, Kim?"

I was still trying to find my voice. She wasn't engaged to Darius.

SHE WASN'T ENGAGED TO DARIUS.

A massive smile lit across my face and I grabbed her hand. "Where are my manners? Let me look. Oh my, that ring is amazing. You'll have to be careful you don't start a fire with that baby. Why wait for Reid? Why don't we celebrate now? Let me buy you and your friend a drink and bun, whatever you like." I was rambling but my mouth wouldn't stop.

"Have you seen Darius lately?" I asked her. "Only I've tried to call him but there was a fault with his phone."

"Yeah, he said there had been, but it's fixed now, so you should ring him." She replied.

Jax got up to get the drinks and buns leaving us alone.

"I don't know what was going on that night at Beached when you ate with Jett, but it has caused problems for the pack."

"Oh, I didn't realise. I'm sorry."

"Why did you date Jett anyway? Are you serious about him?" Sierra's voice had softened.

I shook my head. "No."

"Look, it's none of my business but you need to be honest with Darius. He's my best friend. If you don't want anything to do with him in a romantic way, that's fine. Just let him down gently okay?"

"I'm going to ask him to meet me, so I can explain."

"Great." She smiled at me. Fuck, I was beginning to like the bitch now. "Well, thank you for the coffee and cake. I'd better go back to my friend now."

I took out my phone and scrolled through to Darius'
number and typed him a message.

**Kim: I demand you meet with me so I can
explain everything. Stop being an arse, Darius
Wild.**

Now I just had to wait.

CHAPTER

Six

Shelley

I was in my office—alone.

Thank fucking God.

The last four months had been a crazy whirlwind. I decided to write bullet points on the notepad on my desk so I could try to get my head around everything.

- Discover supernaturals exist.
- Meet and fall in love with a 126-year-old vampire.
- Discover your mother is a witch.
- Find out you have witch powers.
- Discover father is a wyvern.
- Inherit wyvern powers.
- Be informed that your future child shall be the most powerful ruler of Withernsea which started out as a place called Wyvernsea.
- Marry the vampire.
- Discover the ghost of your vampire husband's mother lives in your new home.
- Have to defeat Satan.
- Find out you're pregnant.
- Vampire husband decides this is a good time to redecorate and turn the farm into a Bed and Breakfast.

I think that was all. I stared at the list. There was no wonder I was having a little meltdown moment right now.

On top of this, the dating agency business needed attention, and I was worried about my best friend. I knew Kim's past, knew about her awful father and why she was so hesitant to commit herself to a relationship. Headstrong, stubborn, and impulsive, my bestie had made some rash choices of late and was now living with the consequences.

But picking dates off her work computer as she had with Jett had been a step too far.

One minute she did something crazy like this, the next she rocked up with big ideas for the place like the awesome plan to bring Lucy in. I really did believe that Kim needed a steady influence in her life. She didn't have parents or siblings around and despite my best intentions, with work and my personal life getting ever busier, I wasn't able to be there for her all the time like I could when I was single. The time when I didn't have to look out for Withernsea, when I was just a normal resident and could have a piss in peace without a ghost floating in to tell me some gossip she'd heard, or a husband coming to make sure I was okay.

Thank fuck he slept all day, so I was able to spend the majority of my work hours in peace. Well, as peaceful as it got around here, bearing in mind we'd had Frankie hanging around for months and now we had Lucy. I didn't know what her earth angel duties were about—she couldn't say—but I hoped they didn't have repercussions on my decision to let her have an office here.

The reason I had peace and quiet today was that Lucy and Kim were sorting through all the crap in the old staff room. I'd said I didn't know if dust could affect vampire babies and so they'd agreed to keep me well out of it.

The only thing I was allergic to right now was drama.

I sat back in my chair and closed my eyes.

Peace and quiet at long last.

I woke with a stiff neck from being laid back on the office chair. For a few seconds as I came around, I stared at the clock at the bottom of my computer. I'd been out of it for fifty minutes. Swiping my bag off the floor I took out a bottle of O-neg and downed the contents, giving a satisfied belch at the end. What was happening to me and my life? I had to consider being turned into a vampire along with everything else. I think I was about to have a panic attack.

Instead I had a small heart attack when a middle-aged woman with long dark hair with a white stripe zapped into the room.

"Jesus Christ, mother. You can't do that. You're going to spook the baby out of me."

"I detected anxiety in my firstborn. I had to come. What's the matter, sweetheart. Can I help?"

"Yes, you can start by not doing that again, so I manage to stay alive a few years longer."

My mum sat down opposite me. "What's going on, Shelley?"

"I'm stressed. Overloaded. This time last year the most I had to think about was if I had any clean knickers. Now I'm worrying about being turned into a vampire, birthing a healthy child, keeping everyone in Withernsea alive, and my HUSBAND," I began shouting, "starts decorating the house. Like there isn't enough happening! Now there's dust and mess everywhere and I'm not at the nesting stage, mother, NOT EVEN CLOSE."

"Oh dear. I think your pregnancy hormones have kicked in a little, darling."

"You think?" I spat out as I looked around at the papers that had shot off my desk and were falling all around the room. I'd never had a good handle on my powers mixed with my temper.

"As was." I shouted, and they started to lift up and gather back into piles before they floated back down onto my desk. At least I knew how to rectify my disasters now.

"So is there anything I can do to help?"

I sighed. "Seriously, I doubt it. I'm just fed up is all. My life isn't my own any more. Bloody Withernsea. I'm just glad the new Satan's on vacation so there might be a little peace around the town."

"No mother's life is their own anyway. Comes with the commitment. Even though I had to give you up for adoption, I never stopped searching for you or trying to put things in place for when I could come back home."

"What if I'm a useless mother? I mean if there's a supernatural crisis in Withernsea I'll have to deal with it won't I? What if my baby hates me?" I started crying.

My mum rummaged in her bag and passed me a tissue. "Try not to cry, honey, because the blood stains."

"What?" I wiped my eyes. Sure enough my hands were stained in red.

"Oh my God, I can't even cry properly now." I wailed, and the papers went flying around the office again.

"As is!" I yelled.

My mum stood up. "Come on, let's go to Jax's."

"But I've gone off coffee. I mean that really is the Devil's work, it's got to be. Making me go off coffee and doughnuts is the worst evil I've ever encountered."

"Well, I sure need one, so let's go before I suffer death by a thousand paper cuts. Now come here and let me wipe your eyes because you look like one of those statues that weeps blood. We don't want people stood staring at you praying for miracles."

"I don't mind if they pray for me to be able to drink coffee again." I grumbled, but I let her dab at my face and then I stood up grabbing my bag and chucking my notepad and pen in it.

Jax's had people queuing out of the door and was packed inside. Kim had mentioned it, but I'd thought she was over-exaggerating again. I looked at the front of the queue at the new barista. He was sexy, but this was a little bit overkill. Surely the women of Withernsea had seen a sexy man before? I certainly had. Theo was gorgeous. Darius was a hunk. Here at Jax's they were acting like sex-starved women at a male strip club.

I mumbled some words so that to me and my mother everyone else was muted and then I magicked another table leaving all the room with the suggestion that it had been there all along.

"You aren't supposed to use your magic for personal gain." Mum said.

"It's for the safety of these people here, or I might kill them all." I snipped.

Mum tilted her head at me, "Pregnancy hormones really are the pits. Right, stay there while I go queue for my drink." She held up a hand. "No more magic, Shelley."

I had to sit there for twenty minutes while she queued, but rather than find it a hassle, it was bliss. With everyone muted, I could watch all their interactions but not get a headache from the noise. I started to realise how much people gave away with their body posture and mannerisms. There were so many hair flicks and smiles in the new barista's direction. I focused in on him. The way the women were in here I would have thought he was an incubus, but he gave off no supernatural vibe whatsoever. He'd sent in an application form for the agency and I was in the process of inputting his application. Maybe he really was hotter than the coffee and my recent marriage had dulled my attraction switch. That and my current condition.

My mum returned and sat in front of me with a coffee and a chocolate doughnut. I had all on not to leap across the table and pull her hair out.

"Pass me your bag." She said.

"What?"

"Stop questioning and just do it."

She brought out of my bag a flask and a doughnut.

"What on earth?"

"It's a glamour, you idiot. I'm surprised you didn't think of it before. The flask that to you will taste of Jax's coffee, is in fact your bottle of O-neg and your portion of liver will now taste and look like a doughnut."

Why hadn't I thought of that?

Because I'd been too busy drowning in self pity, that's why.

"Mum, you're a genius!" I told her as I bit into my doughnut, the chocolate oozing out of the middle. For the first time in days a beaming smile broke across my face.

My mum took a drink of her own coffee and smiled. "Mmmm, I swear this gets better."

"Thanks, Mum. I needed this."

"I know, honey, you basically sent out a mental SOS."

"Did that happen when you were on the astral plane?"

She shook her head. "No. Until you came into your powers, I couldn't locate you at all. They were the worst years of my life and I thank the powers that be every day now that I was returned to your life."

It was hard to believe that my separation from my parents was due to the fact that my dad had left Lucy for mum, resulting in years in hell for my father, trapped by Lucy when she was a demon, and my mum stuck on the astral plane. I couldn't equate that Lucy to the one I knew now, and that was probably a good thing. There'd been fault on all sides anyway, and it had cost each of them dearly.

"How is Dad?"

"He's fine, lovely. He's spending a lot of time swimming out at the caves. Oh, that reminds me, he says everything in the sea is calm, so you don't need to worry about that anyway. Your father's happy to keep an eye on the water."

"You mean to tell me I have the whole sea to govern as well?"

"Well, of course. You're taking over rule from your father. At some point we'll need to have a coronation and that will be one ceremony on land and another under the water so you can meet your subjects. You'll be their queen."

I necked the coffee. Okay maybe it wasn't able to give me the same effect with it being a glamour, but the blood gave me a buzz and it stopped me from screaming out loud while my mouth was full of liquid.

I picked up my bag and rummaged inside until I found my pen. I placed that and my notebook on the table and added to my list.

Rule the seas of Withernsea and meet supernatural water creatures.

Then for dramatic effect I added in capital letters.

HAVE A NERVOUS BREAKDOWN.

My mother grabbed the notepad and looked down the list. "Oh, honey. Why haven't you told me about all this? I could have helped you. A problem shared is a problem halved after all."

"Not unless you're taking on half my to-do list." I grumbled.

"Let's have a look and see if there's anything I can do." She said, completely ignoring me. I vowed to always listen to my child and attend to their every whim right there and then.

"This isn't a to-do list. It's just a list. We can scratch out half the things on it." She said, picking up my pen.

"Right, 'discover supernaturals exist'. Yes, you discovered it and what? How is that a problem? It's helped you double your business hasn't it?"

"Well, yes."

"Right I'm crossing that off. 'Meet and fall in love with a 126-year-old vampire.' Oh you're madly in love, oh how life sucks. Well, your husband does, at your neck. I'm crossing that off." She struck through my writing. "'Discover your mother is a witch. Find out you have witch powers. Discover father is a wyvern'. Yes, undoubtedly this will take some getting used to, along with the next one about your powers and being the current ruler of Withernsea. But we are here to help you now. Before you didn't have your parents around you, so think of it as a good thing that you're reunited with your mother and father."

She took a sip of coffee. "'Be informed your future child shall be the most powerful ruler of Withernsea which started out as a place called Wyvernsea'. Well, you have the advantage of knowing your baby's future. What about mums who don't know their future treasured offspring will grow up to be a serial killer, or a thief? Yours will be powerful and held in high esteem by the community. Boo hoo."

My mother had a point. I was being a mardy arse,

wasn't I? I took the pen off her and scratched a couple of things off the list.

~~Marry the vampire.~~
Discover the ghost of your vampire husband's mother lives in your new home.
~~Have to defeat Satan.~~
~~Find out you're pregnant.~~
Vampire husband decides this is a good time to redecorate and turn the farm into a Bed and Breakfast.

"'Discover the ghost of your vampire husband's mother lives in your new home'. Well, a lot of women have the mother-in-law from hell, yours is just floating around earth, be thankful. You've a permanent babysitter on hand, and she can help with the bed and breakfast."

"I don't think seeing a ghost is going to help business much."

"Shelley, make it supernaturals only. It won't hurt to suggest to human enquirers that you're full. I know Theo's excited about his new business venture and it must be difficult for him to get his teeth into something that excites him after 127 years on earth. Gosh, that came out wrong didn't it?" She said as we both burst into guffaws of laughter.

"Aw thanks, Mum. I've been ruminating about things that are in the past and things in the future that are beyond my control. Not only have you helped me with that, but you even sorted my coffee and doughnut problem. I love you, Mum. You're amazing." It was the first time I'd said the words to her since I'd found out who she was and had started the process of getting to know her. I watched as my mum's face crumpled and she began to sob. "I'm so sorry I had to leave you, Shelley. It was the biggest mistake of my life and I suffered every day."

"It's in the past, Mum. Let's just enjoy the here and now, shall we? That's what I'm going to do from now on." I said, and then we heard the coffee shop door burst open and a voice screamed, "We're all doomed."

CHAPTER

Seven

Shelley

My jaw dropped open as Ebony almost fell through the doorway before she practically bounced off the nearest table. My mum and I ran towards her holding a side of her each and steered her to our table where I made another chair subtly appear and plopped her onto it. This chair had arms so she couldn't fall off, given that she was rip-roaringly drunk.

"Ebony, how much vodka have you had?" I whisper-hissed.

"I don't remember. I don't remember anything." Her eyes went wide. "I got to the boutique this morning for eight, and then it's all blank, and my visions have stopped."

"Well, duh, isn't that why you have all the vodka?"

Her hands flailed around her face. "I drink to lessen them but they've gone. My mama always said if they went then that meant major evil was around. I can't protect people right now with no visions. What if you all die?"

Ebony then headbutted the table as she passed clean out.

Jax came running over. My mute spell had dropped the minute I'd started talking to Ebony, and I was more than aware of the gossip and stares happening around us. I picked up my mobile phone.

"Kim? Stop tidying, we have an emergency at Jax's. No, the coffee hasn't run out. It's Ebony, there's something wrong with her. Can you or Lucy mind her boutique? Lock the office up and get down here will you, quick as you can?"

I carefully lifted my friend's head up to make sure she was just passed out and hadn't broken her nose or anything, on her face's date with the table top.

"Can you get some really strong coffee for her, Jax?"

"Sure, coming right up." Jax went over to some customers seated on a sofa. After she'd talked to them they got up and came over to us, a look of concern on their faces.

"We're gonna help you move your friend over to the sofa so she can lie down with her feet up." One of them said. "Then we'll have your table."

"Thanks so much," I said, and I went to help move Ebony.

"Hold it right there! You shouldn't lift anything in your condition." Yelled my gobshite best friend from the doorway. She then realised she'd announced my unannounced pregnancy to half the female population of Withernsea. "With your bad back." She shouted louder. "The doctor said you weren't to move anything with your BAD BACK."

"If only I had Ebony's foresight I could mute your damn mouth." I said to Kim as she came over. At least she went to the gym and so was good at helping move the dead weight of our friend.

Finally after some huffing and puffing Ebony was laid on the sofa with her feet elevated above her head. She was starting to come around and started groaning. On my mother's advice we murmured a spell suggesting that the other customers in the cafe had had enough coffee and cake and they gathered their coats and left.

"Oh dear, Ebony's drama has scared off my customers. I

hope they come back." Jax said, unaware that anyone in Withernsea had supernatural powers.

"I'm sure they'll be back soon. At least it gives you a chance to get cleared up and have a breather."

"Oh why am I thinking about my customers? It's Ebony I should be worried about." She shouted over to Seth. "While it's quiet why don't you take a break, Seth?"

He removed his apron and came around from the back of the counter. "Is there anything I can do? I'm so sorry I couldn't help move her but I was stuck behind the counter serving." He looked around. "It's so strange how everyone left like that. Can I help at all?"

"We're okay here, Seth. Thank you. Either get your break or if you could help by tidying up..." Jax said.

"I'll clear up."

"I'll help you." My mum told him.

"Thanks, Margret." Jax said. "Help yourself to anything from behind the counter."

"Is Seth included?" Kim smirked.

"If you fancy a sandwich or a bun or anything." Jax added.

I took a baby wipe out of my bag and started wiping Ebony's brow with it.

"Aww, look at you, you're already being all..."

I glared at Kim.

"Efficient." She exhaled. "You are so, so, efficient."

Ebony continued to come around, and we gave her some sips of water and then strong coffee. I decided she wasn't in a fit state to stay by herself back home. "Listen, we're going to stay here for a while. Just here on the sofa and then when it gets to four o'clock I will call Theo and ask him to take us to mine."

Ebony started to protest.

"No. You're coming to our house and that's that, until we work out you're okay. We've loads of room. I'm not leaving you on your own until your visions are back. You can't carry on like this anyway," I said looking at her. "I'm going to ring the *doctor*." I emphasised the word doctor so that Ebony knew I meant the one who helped supes.

"Frankie." Ebony said. "Frankie might be able to help me."

"Okay, we'll call Frankie. Again, we'll have to wait until later." Frankie used to be a physician at the local hospital before he became a vampire so as long as we waited until he was awake he could well be able to help Ebony.

I looked at my friend. To say she was dark skinned she looked pale. I was so used to her dramatic behaviour I'd never really stopped to think about what it was doing to her mental and physical health. There must be something I could do to help her live with her visions because from what I'd seen today if not they were going to slowly kill her.

Theo had to use his car rather than whizz here by vampire super speed. Luckily we didn't live too far away. Ebony had spent most of the afternoon sleeping. Theo walked in and picked her up like she weighed the same as a Barbie doll. "Subtle, husband, subtle." I whispered knowing his vampire hearing would pick it up. He started to act like he was struggling with her weight. "Let's get you to the car." He said. Then he stood stock still and stared at Seth.

"I don't believe we've met." He said, and no word of a lie while he was holding my friend he let one hand go and held his other out to Seth. God help me.

"Seth Whittaker." Seth said, shaking his hand. "I'm the new barista."

"Oh, my wife didn't mention there was a new barista. Good to meet you." He said and then stared into Seth's eyes. "You will never find my wife attractive, when you see her you will think of your grandmother naked."

"Theo!" I yelled.

Seth was staring into space as the compelling took place. I knew as soon as it had worked because he glanced over to us and then heaved. Bloody insecure vampire husbands.

"Let's get out of here before someone gets hurt, and I mean you." I yelled at Theo. He put his hand back on Ebony and pretended to struggle again.

"Take that image out of Seth's mind." I mimed to my mum, who nodded. Otherwise poor Seth was going to be a basketcase.

When we got back to the farm, Mary, Theo's mother, greeted us. Mary was a ghost but could solidify while ever she could summon the energy. "Who have we here?" She said. "And I don't think drugging people is the way to get boarders."

"It's my friend Ebony. She's not feeling well so I've brought her here so we can take care of her."

"Oh, the poor love. I'll try to put the kettle on." Mary bustled off.

"Come on, Ebony, let's get you settled on the sofa." Theo helped me get her there and then I sent him to the kitchen to help his mum to make a lot of black coffee.

Ebony looked up at me from the sofa. "I'm so sorry,

Shelley, for causing all this trouble. I panicked when my visions went."

"It's probably that you're so tired, Ebs. I really do think we need to find a way other than vodka for you to deal. Now just lay back for a moment while I phone Frankie, okay?"

She nodded, and I settled a couple of cushions underneath her head and neck and she closed her eyes again.

~

"Frankie, I need your help."

"Anytime, lovely. What can I do for you?"

"Can you come over to the farm? Ebony is having a lot of trouble handling her visions and now she says they've disappeared. She turned up to Jax's so drunk she was knocking furniture over."

"Oh shit. And you say the visions have left her?"

"Yeah."

"Okay, babes. Give me some time to look into that and then I'll come over. It could be late."

"That doesn't matter." Since I'd been drinking blood I'd found my body clock was changing, and I was going to bed and getting up later. It was giving me a taste of what would probably happen when I was turned.

I ended the call and sighed. I hoped we could help her.

"Wife. You need to rest now for an hour. It's been a stressful afternoon for you. Ebony is asleep and mum is looking after her." Theo grabbed my hand and pulled me in the direction of the stairs.

"I'm wide awake. Theo, I don't need a rest." I complained.

"Oh even better." Theo said and still pulled on my hand.

"I need to look after my friend."

Mary floated out into the hallway. "Love, go upstairs, because you know what men are like when they've got the horn on, can't leave us alone until they're spent. I'm okay here. Listen, I'll make a ghostly wail outside your room if you're needed. I need to practice it as when the Bed and Breakfast is open I'm going to start haunting the customers. Ghost sightings can bring in good trade."

I placed a hand on my temple. She was going to haunt the customers? It was definitely a good idea to stick with boarding supernaturals only or the incidences of death by heart attack at our establishment could be significantly higher than average amongst other b&bs in the area.

She floated back off, and I looked at my husband. "So you have the horn, huh?"

"I fear if I wasn't already dead the need would kill me. It's like my groin is trying to burst out like the creatures in that film Alien."

"Well, I guess you'd better take me upstairs then."

Theo wasn't joking. He quickly stripped off his trousers and his cock sprung out like a jack in a box. After shedding the rest of his clothes at vamp speed he helped me out of the rest of mine.

"I cannot wait to be sunk inside your depths." He announced making the corner of my mouth turn up in amusement. Sometimes it took some getting used to that my husband was 127.

He walked over to our chest of drawers and opening the top one pulled out a pair of handcuffs.

"Theo! What are you up to, you filthy boy?"

"I have been acquainting myself with that series all you women like, so lie on the bed. Now. Do as you're told."

Hmmm, not quite sure 'do as you're told' was the usual Dom command but my pussy went slick anyway at the thought of a little playtime so I climbed onto the bed.

Theo climbed alongside me and leaning over he grabbed my wrist and clicked a cuff around it, fastening the other to a bedpost at the top of the bed.

"I could only get one pair and I need to secure your other wrist. Ah, my tie." He said, climbing off the bed and going through his discarded clothes. He restrained my other wrist and then sat at my feet.

"Oh lovely wife. What shall I do to you now?" He winked.

He licked, nibbled and kissed from my feet all the way up to near my core. His cool touch set my body to goose bump and by the time his cool tongue met my clit I was in a frenzy of need. "Oh my God, yes."

My back arched, and the chain rattled on one wrist while the tie tightened on the other.

Theo continued to lick me and suck on me while his right hand travelled upwards to tease my nipples, which pebbled under his touch.

"Please, Theo. I need you." I was desperate to have him inside me.

"If it wasn't for our guest, I would keep you in here all evening. Alas, I suppose I should move things along." He sighed, climbing up my body and rubbing along my slit with the tip of his hard dick. I spread my legs wider, and he pushed inside.

"Ooohhh, yes, yes."

Theo pushed deeper, and I raised my hips matching him thrust for thrust. Being pregnant was making me even more horny than I usually was for my sexy husband. I hoped he was going to bite my neck because that made me come so hard I'd see stars. He nuzzled my neck, and I nuzzled him back.

And as we came together, the bite was amazing. My pussy climaxed so hard around Theo's cock I was surprised it didn't cut off his circulation.

Then Theo pushed me back away from him and withdrew feeling at his neck. A look of horror on his face.

He pulled his hand away, and I saw blood on his fingertips. My vision travelled to his neck where I saw puncture wounds. My mouth felt funny and as I ran my tongue around it I felt the two protrusions.

I had fangs?

I. HAD. FANGS.

I tried to feel my teeth with my hands but of course my arms were restrained.

"Whath the fuck isth happening, Theo? Why do I haveth fangs?"

"You bit me. You bit me!" Theo said. "How can you have fangs?"

"Justh geth me outh these cuffths." I was beginning to panic now.

Theo undid the tie and then looked at the handcuffs and froze.

"Whath?" I glared at him. "Whath up? Leth me go."

"Erm, when I borrowed the handcuffs, I forgot to get the keys." Theo looked at the floor while biting on his lip. Then feeling blood running down his neck he licked his finger and ran it over the puncture wounds sealing them.

"Then cuth them off or go backth to the shop."

"I didn't get them from a shop. I kind of knew Darius wasn't working and so I just 'popped' there for a second to borrow them."

"They're Dariusth?"

Theo looked sheepish.

"Didth he know you borroweth them?"

"I was going to take them straight back."

I tried to demonstrate my frustration by letting my head flop back against the pillows. Here I was, handcuffed to the bed by a were shifter policeman's handcuffs while I seemed to have grown fangs, and in the meantime there was a guest downstairs who needed my help.

"Go geth them." I screamed.

CHAPTER

Eight

Kim

Lucy was running Ebony's shop until closing and that left me, Seth and Margret helping Jax to cope with the swarm of people who descended once Shelley and Theo had taken Ebony home. At closing time we were happy to swing the open/closed sign around and lock the door.

"Jax, you'll need some more staff at this rate."

"I know." She stretched out her body and rolled her neck. "It's killing me. I just don't know what's caused it."

"There's probably been a mention in a magazine or on Twitter or something." Seth suggested. "These things happen and go viral. It'll settle down in a day or two, I'm sure."

"I wish I knew the future." Jax sucked on her top lip. "If I knew it was going to stay busy I'd hire but I don't want to do that if it might stop. Trust Ebony's visions to stop now. I could have asked her to read my palm."

"Well, I'm not going anywhere." Seth said.

"You've been amazing, but now go home." She pushed him towards the door, or rather she tried to, but her five foot waif like frame versus his six foot muscular one meant he didn't move. In fact if he hadn't have been looking he probably would have thought a fly had landed on him.

"Well, I'd better get back. Dylan will be wondering where I am." Margret bid us goodbye and left.

"I'm just going to ring and see how Ebony's doing." I told the other two.

It rang a few times and then a faint voice came onto the line. "Helllooooo."

"Mary? It's Kim. Is Shelley or Theo there?"

"No, lovey, they're in bed. Can I help you at all? You'll have to be quick though I keep fading in and out."

I shook my head then realised she couldn't see me.

"In bed? What about Ebony?"

"She's fast asleep on the sofa so I'm keeping an eye on her. My son came home acting very possessive and whisked Shelley upstairs. I don't know what happened while they were out but I'm surprised he wasn't beating his chest or dragging her around by her hair. He'd gone all caveman."

I laughed knowing he'd met Seth.

"Okay, well, as long as everything seems settled. I'm making my way home now as I need to get ready to go out later. Tell Shelley to call my mobile if she needs me."

"Will do."

"Oh." Seth had puckered up his delectable lips and scrunched up his nose. "I was going to see if you wanted to come for a quick drink? Only I'm knackered and could sink a pint. I didn't fancy being there on my own."

I had to admit that with the nerves hitting my body about my upcoming date with Darius, a drink was exactly what I needed. One couldn't hurt, could it?

"Sounds good to me. Let's go. I'll take you to The Marine. Have you been there yet?"

"No."

We nodded at Jax. "Do you fancy a drink, Jax?" I asked her.

"Nah, I'm buggered. I want my sofa. Enjoy yourselves you two. Have a drink for me."

It was a ten minute walk to the pub which gave me a chance to try to get to know Seth better. I told myself it would help me find him a date but really I was just a nosy bitch.

"So, are you from Withernsea? I don't recall seeing you around here?" *And I would have because you're one hot fucker.*

"No, I was born in Hull. I just decided a couple of weeks ago that I was fed up and fancied a change. I was sick of going to Cleethorpes so I looked what other beaches were close and chose this one. Thought I'd do a few months casual work and then go back to Hull and my mundane life."

"I bet your life isn't really mundane."

"I'm an Assistant Manager at a supermarket. Or rather I was before I handed in my notice and came here. They've promised me a job on return, but said it will be most likely back on the shop floor. I can't seem to care." He looked down at me, "how about you?"

"Lived here all my life. Met Shelley when we went speed dating. We were supposed to find dates, but I found a best friend instead. Been working at the dating agency now for almost a year and a half. Got a promotion to run-" I was about to say the supernatural side. Shit, my mouth had been trying to get me in trouble all day. "To help run the agency with Shelley, now she's all married. Plus the agency has got a lot busier of late. So that's it. I live in a house on my own and at the moment I'm happy that way. So you said you were divorced?"

"Yes. I'm renting a flat above a chippy right now. I'm going to get fat with a chippy below me, and a job at a coffee shop with the best buns I've ever tasted."

I looked over his buff body and the thought of tasting his buns crossed my mind. The firm ones packed inside the arse of his jeans. I really needed to calm my libido. Jeez, I'd bet I was ovulating. I was like a bitch on heat when I was halfway through my cycle. I'd need to be careful not to try to mount Darius when I saw him.

"Yes, I agree. Jax has the best buns and the best coffee. If she ever tries to shut up shop, you'll find me on the nearest bridge."

We reached the pub and went inside. Luckily there were a few spare tables. Seth chose one near a window and we sat down. "What would you like to drink?"

"Erm, half a beer please. You choose which one, they have a lot of guest beers on here."

He nodded and went to the bar.

Returning with my half pint and a pint for himself, he sat down opposite me. He picked up his glass and chinked it against mine. "Cheers." He said.

"Cheers." I replied.

He picked up a food menu. "If you want to eat here, it's my treat. I've nothing to rush home for."

"Oh actually I'm going out." I told him.

"Oh." He said, placing his menu down on the table. "Anywhere nice?"

I was about to tell him about my dinner date when my phone buzzed with a text notification. Opening my bag, I rooted around, upending tissues, pens, my purse, a small hand gel, and some painkillers. I needed one of those handbag compartment things to help organise me, I thought and then realised that there was one right at the very bottom of the bag and I'd just been throwing things on top of it. Eventually, I located my mobile phone underneath it and lifted it out.

Darius: An emergency has come up so I can't make it. I'll be in touch.

I sighed. Huh, I'd bet there was no such emergency, and he was just putting me off. When would I get it into my thick head that he wasn't interested anymore? What I needed was a nice human male to date and oh look, here was one right in front of me.

"My plans cancelled so if the offer of dinner is still on, then yes, I'd love to stay and eat."

"Great." Seth put his hand on top of mine. "Not that your plans have fallen through, but that you can stay for dinner." He passed me a copy of the menu. "So my treat."

"No, I'll pay my own way." I told him.

"Not a chance. Look you get them next time."

Next time?

I sat back, placing my mobile phone back in my bag, and picked up my drink. "I think I'll have a burger and fries. You'd better get a salad though, fat boy."

He tilted his head, raised an eyebrow and then slowly lifted his tee showing me a six pack, then he rippled his abdomen.

I needed to pour my drink over my head to cool me down.

"Think I'm okay a bit yet." He said, winking, then he went to the bar.

I watched his buns move.

Fuck Darius. I was moving on.

The evening was fun, and we caught a taxi home, calling at my house first.

"Just a moment." Seth said to the taxi driver, and he ran around my side and opened the door for me.

"How very gentlemanly of you." I said.

"I do my best." He replied. "On a first date anyway. Can't promise to be so gentlemanly on a second."

I looked up at him. "Is that what this was? A date?"

"We spent time together and shared food." Seth shrugged as he followed me up the path to my door.

"I do that with my friends, I'm not dating them."

Then I wasn't speaking anymore because my lips were otherwise engaged. Seth's warm mouth met my own in a sweet, chaste kiss.

"Thank you for a lovely evening." He said, walking backwards down the path. "And we kissed, so I think that most definitely makes it a date."

I watched as he climbed back inside the taxi and it drove away. I wasn't sure what I felt about the evening. Mainly as I was supposed to be out with Darius, not Seth, and I'd thought we were just grabbing a bite to eat as mates. Now I seemed to have a new boyfriend. Shelley was going to murder me for dating another guy off our own books. Was I actually dating him? I needed some time to think about everything. My mind was so confused.

And then I saw him, standing across the street.

Darius.

He shook his head at me. He must have seen everything.

"Darius, wait!" I yelled, running down the path.

But he was a were, and even without shifting, he could

still outrun me by a mile. He was gone before I'd reached the edge of the path, leaving me with nothing but the fading roar of a motorbike engine.

There was no wonder Ebony was losing her mind with my antics. I was driving myself crazy.

CHAPTER

Nine

Darius

A few hours earlier...

Alyssa kept smiling at me from her position on the sofa as I paced around the floor.

"So what time are you meeting her?"

"Who?"

"Your date?"

"Who says I have a date?" I shrugged my shoulders.

"You've shaved, smell to high heaven of Lynx, you're in your favorite jeans, and you can't stand still."

She tilted her head at me. "Oh my God, it's with Kim isn't it? That's why you're in such a state."

"I am not in a state." I growled.

"So what time are you meeting her?" She asked again.

"Eight at Hanifs."

"Yeah, Boi." She stood up at raised her hand for a high-five. Teenagers were so frikking weird.

"Why are you so interested in my love life?"

"Cos when it comes to you getting a mate it means mum stops looking at what I'm doing."

I narrowed my eyes. "And what are you doing?"

She gave a big fake smile. "Nothing at all, big brother. I'm being my angelic self and behaving perfectly."

I placed my palm to my face and rubbed at my eyes. "I can't think about what you're up to right now."

"Exactly." She mimed a mike drop and said the word, "Boom."

I started pacing again, then found her in front of me staring at me again.

"Oh my God, what, Alyssa?"

"Undo your top button. You look too formal on top. Now roll up your sleeves." She stood back appraising me. "That's better. Now take your hair out of that man bun. That's so last year. In fact, we have two hours before your date and time to fix it. Let's see if Zara is free to cut it."

"I'm ready. The man bun lives another day. Now sod off and leave me alone."

Alyssa rolled her eyes. "If you've been dreaming about her undoing your hair and running her hands through it I'm gonna barf."

"Out."

"It's my living room as well as yours, dufus."

My phone ringing stopped further arguments. Theo's name flashed up on the screen.

"Hey, pal. How's it going?"

"I've got an emergency. I need your help."

My posture stiffened. "Police help, or friend help?"

"Erm..."

"Theo, tell me. I can't help unless I know."

There was a pause. "Alas, I feel this may affect our future friendship, your trust in me."

"You've killed someone, haven't you?"

"No."

"There's been a murder? Can I come, can I come? Is there lots of blood? I watch Game of Thrones. I promise I'll be quiet."

"Just a minute." I said down the phone, then I turned to my sister. "There hasn't been a murder, now go and have underage sex or drink too much and just get from under my feet."

"Okay, bro. Very open-minded of you. I'll be sure to tell Ma I had your permission when I'm a barefoot, preggo lush."

My mind was going to explode soon between delinquent sisters, panicked friends, and my upcoming date. I decided to leave my sister in the living room and head up to my own room.

"Right, Theo. I'm back. You need to tell me what's going on."

"Verily, I may have happened upon your handcuffs, looked after them for a time and forgotten the key."

All of a sudden it became crystal clear.

"You rogue. Well I never, Theo Landry. We'll talk about the fact you went through my belongings without asking later. Right now, on a scale of one to ten how mad is Shelley?"

"Three thousand and twenty six, as a rough estimate."

"I'm on my way."

When I arrived at the farm, Theo greeted me at the door looking even paler than his usual vampire self if that were at all possible.

He clasped his hands in front of him. "Before you enter, you need to be appraised of the full situation."

"Okay..."

"There is a seer on the sofa. She's hungover because she has lost her visions."

"Right."

"My mum is looking after her. Now you haven't met my mother yet but I think she will be making herself known soon enough. She's currently watching over Ebony."

"Okay."

"Frankie and Margret are both on their way over to help with another delicate matter. I would be grateful for your opinion on whether I free my beloved wife now or later."

"Why would you not free her now?"

"Please follow me upstairs." He said and began to walk up the first step.

"Erm, not sure about coming into your chamber, Theo. Isn't your missus kinda tied up?"

"I have put a robe around her. Only her wrists and ankles are on show, and... well, her mouth."

"Come on then." I checked my watch. I was due to meet Kim in an hour, so the sooner I was out of here the better.

When I walked into their room, it was like a scene from a horror movie. Shelley was pulling at her handcuffed wrist, her mouth covered in red blood, and oh my fucking God were they fangs? She actually hissed as Theo walked in the room.

"Get me out of these handcuffs now, you bastard. Oh my God, you brought Darius? How am I supposed to show my face in front of him again, you utter twat?"

"Wife, you aren't lisping anymore. Are you getting used to your teeth?"

"Bite me, you motherfucker."

The image of a woman floated into the room before solidifying in front of me. I blinked twice and when I opened my eyes, there was a woman dressed in a long white gown, with dark hair in a bun standing in front of me.

"I assure you there was none of that going on between me and my son, young lady." She stopped in front of me and froze in place, her mouth open. Her image trembled and then she moved and dropped to a curtsy in front of me. Looking up from under her lashes she spoke. "I don't believe we have met. I'm Mary. Could I be of assistance to you at all? A drink perhaps, or I could launder your clothes?"

"My clothes are clean."

"We could dirty them?" She giggled.

"Mother, behave yourself." Theo shouted.

Mother!

"I do apologise. She's been dead a long time and so hasn't seen many men in quite some years."

"Or had sex." Mary added.

Theo held his forehead. "So, on the rare occasion I bring a male to the house, she gets a little... excitable."

Mary winked at me and did a call me mime.

"Mother, we already have been blacklisted from Domino's Pizza delivery and they'll no longer deliver newspapers to the house. Could you please gather yourself?"

Mary huffed. "I'll go back to Ebony."

"Are you all quite finished?" Spat Shelley, a few drops of blood splattering from her mouth. "Only I could use some help over here."

"Do you see my predicament now?" Theo asked. "Do I keep her restrained until her mother arrives? She's very volatile and unpredictable."

"Unfasten me, you wanker, or I'll cut off your balls when I eventually get free."

I stepped forward. "Shelley. Shelley, are you in there?"

She gave me the side-eye. "Where else would I be, Darius?"

"Oh." I said surprised. "I thought you were, well, possessed."

Theo sighed. "No, this is just my wife in a bad mood."

"Shelley. I will undo the cuffs, but only if you promise that no violence will occur. Your wrists will be numb anyway. While I do that, Theo, get some warm water and a flannel so Shelley can clean her mouth."

Theo nodded rather enthusiastically at being able to leave the room.

I walked to the right-hand side of the bed and undid the cuff from her wrist. She pulled her arm towards her and rubbed it frantically.

"My husband is an idiot."

"He is, a total idiot, but it's because he's blinded with love for you. The dingbat nicked my handcuffs to please you. Now I'm gonna be having words about his invasion of my space, but he'd have never have done anything like that a year ago. He's just trying to please you."

Shelley folded her arms over herself and exhaled.

"I suppose."

"Look, when I eventually find my mate, I will make acts toward her that are out of nature. I will cook for her when I have hardly ever been in a kitchen in my life because to feed our mate is something we are duty bound to do. Once she is my mate, I will learn to cook so I can cherish her when she's with cub."

Shelley fastened her gaze on mine. She was calming down but her body posture was still taut. I was used to dealing with unpredictable behaviour in my line of work. If she launched she'd be cuffed again and it wouldn't be for sexy times. "Aren't you meeting my friend tonight?"

I looked at my watch. "Shit. Shit. I need to get out of here."

Shelley put a hand on her stomach. "Oh God, I don't feel so good."

I rushed to her side. "Is it the baby?"

And then she puked. Red spray all across my shirt and jeans.

At that moment Theo walked in with a flannel and a small bowl of water. Shelley was looking mortified, and I was trying not to be sick myself.

"Oh, I'll be back again in a moment... with a bucket." Theo announced, leaving the room once more.

And that's when I found myself sat with a towel wrapped around me in a guest room, while Theo laundered my clothes as nothing of his would fit my wide frame. I texted Kim to cancel, knowing there was no way my clothes would be ready on time. It would just have to be rescheduled, it couldn't be helped. I put that it was an emergency, so she'd know I wasn't messing her around. She knew I worked in law enforcement. She'd think it was that. I was bitterly disappointed. I'd wanted to clear the air and take her on a date, see if she really was the woman I'd like to eventually make my mate.

In the meantime I kept having Mary pop in to 'see if I was alright'. Trouble was she never looked at my face when she said it. She might only look in her thirties, but she was still my friend's mother, ghost or not. It was weird. I think Shelley or Kim needed to find a date for her. There must be other unsettled ghosts around the place.

While I waited for my clothes, I heard voices from

downstairs and presumed Frankie or Margret had arrived to see what to do about Shelley and the appearance of fangs. I was in no rush to go say hi. The further away I was from Shelley's pregnant 'Mouth Vesuvius', the better. I'd just stay in this guest room and lament my lost date.

Part of me wondered if it was a sign. Before Ebony's predictions, I'd thought the idea of fate was a bag of shit, but when Ebony started telling me Kim was my destiny, I'd wanted to believe it. I'd been hooked on the woman since I first set eyes on her despite the fact she was cocky as fuck. You see, I felt it was surface bravado and that underneath there were layers to get through to find the real Kim. I wanted to peel back those layers and peel off her clothes.

"Ooops." Mary giggled, and I realised my thoughts had produced a hard-on which was tenting the towel.

Fuck my life.

When my clothes had finally been returned, and I'd dressed again, I headed down to the living room. It was a benefit that the room was large because Shelley, Theo, Margret, Ebony, and Frankie, were sat in there, and now there was me and Mary to add to the party.

"Mother. You're fading. Go rest." Theo ordered.

"Yes, love. I was just about to say goodnight. It's been a busy day. Goodnight all."

"Thank you for caring for me when I was indisposed." Ebony said in her cut-glass accent.

"Not a problem at all, lovey. I hope they get you all sorted. Okay people, I'm out of here. I look forward to seeing you all again under better circumstances. You too, big boy."

I felt my face burn.

"Darius is fated to end up with Kim. It's been seen in Ebony's visions. Sorry, Mary." Shelley told her while wearing a sympathetic look. It appeared her fangs had gone.

"Oh. What a shame. I'll just have to order some more takeaways and see who turns up." She said and then she disappeared.

"She burned herself out." Shelley said in explanation. "She'll be back in a few hours."

"I must apologise for my mother's behaviour. It is most unusual. She was never like this in life."

"Yeah, her death gave her a new lease of life. Weird or what?" Shelley said to him.

"Alas. No one should have to witness their mother trying to flirt with their friends."

"So have we found anything out about your fangs, or why Ebony's visions have stopped?"

Frankie stood up from the sofa and began pacing. "Shelley's fangs are easily explained. It's an anomaly. She's not turning into a vampire. It's the fact she's carrying a part-vampire child. The child is thirsty for blood and so it has caused a temporary genetic change that means Shelley can grow fangs in order to procure the blood. Obviously, she needs to be careful that pregnancy cravings don't cause her to drain anyone. If she increases her intake, the cravings will be kept at bay and everything should be fine. Once the baby is born, Shelley will no longer grow fangs. Of course she's considering been turned soon anyway, but we'll cross that bridge when we come to it. For now mother and baby are doing well."

"And Ebony?"

"No one knows." Ebony looked up at me. "I shouldn't have lost them. I thought it meant I might die, but Frankie says that's a myth, that seers don't lose their visions, unless someone is doing this deliberately to me."

"So someone could be trying to block them?"

"Yes. But I don't know who or why, so unless something happens to reveal if that's the case, there's nothing I can do. In the meantime I shall take a recuperative break. It will be nice to be sober for a time. I'm having a visions and vodka detox."

"Frankie and myself are going to research if there's some kind of spell or potion we can make so that Ebony no longer has to reach for the vodka. It's not healthy and they're preventing Ebony from having a life of her own." Shelley reached across to Ebony and placed a hand on her arm. "I've been a crap friend. I'd not thought about the fact that you'd not been able to rest and had been relying more and more on alcohol."

"Oh, darling. It's not your fault. That's the life of a seer. It's a fact that many do not live until old age. Suicide rates are high in my kind."

"That's not happening to you, Ebs. No way."

"Right, so we think there could be someone in Withernsea tampering with your visions? Putting up a block?"

"It's a possibility." Frankie nodded.

"I'll do some investigating. See if there's anyone new to the area, who's been in close proximity to Ebony. I'll open a 'black file' police report."

Frankie gasped "What has her ethnicity to do with this? I did not have you for a racist, Darius Wild."

Ebony burst out laughing. "It's what the supernatural cases are called, Frankie. Darius has to be careful being around human colleagues."

"Oh." Frankie looked sheepish.

Ebony stood and hugged him. "Thank you for looking out for me. It's much appreciated."

White feathers rained down over them both and the next minute Lucy appeared in the room. "Hey all. I've been sent here so you must be talking about something connected with my earth angel job. Care to enlighten me?"

"Long story short. I grew fangs, but it's because of the baby. Ebony's visions are blocked and that could be because someone is interfering with them."

"Oh they are." Lucy said, perching on a sofa arm.

"Pardon?" We all said at once.

"It would be helpful if you could explain what's going on?" I told her.

She shrugged her shoulders. "Sorry, no can do. Angel vows. I'm on it though, you'll just all have to trust me."

Trust the recent Manager of Hell?

That was a new one.

This lot had exhausted me and the fact my date with Kim had been postponed itched at my skin. I looked at my watch. It was half past ten. I decided to call around to see her. Just to explain I'd been with her friends and that I wasn't playing games. Enough of that had gone on between us. It was time for honesty. I said goodbye to everyone, got on my motorcycle and drove down to her house. My bike was powerful and made a lot of noise, so being considerate I parked it at the end of the estate and walked down. There was a taxi outside the front of her house with its engine running and as I walked closer, I saw that Kim was standing outside her house--with another man. On closer inspection I saw it was the new guy from the coffee shop. Well she didn't waste any time. And then he kissed her. No more than a quick brush against her lips, but he kissed my mate. I felt my wolf churn inside me and had to resist the change as my body trembled with the urge to shift. He got in the taxi and it passed me as I stood on the pavement. As her eyes watched the taxi move away, I noted the moment she saw me standing there. She froze.

"Darius." She shouted.

I couldn't fight my change any longer. My wolf thrashed and twisted inside me to get free. So I ran, jumped on my bike and sped away for the woods. I needed to let loose with my animal. There was no way I wanted my human thoughts right now. I wanted to tear the ground up beneath my feet, and howl until every bit of the frustration had left me.

CHAPTER

Ten

Kim

I'd not slept well. My mind churning with thoughts of yesterday. I'd decided against texting Darius, or trying to call him. There was only seeing him face-to-face now that could sort out this mess. Even worse, despite my tiredness, my day would be free of Jax's coffee, because there was no way I was stepping foot in there. The last person I wanted to see was Seth. Not today.

Seth was lovely, but he was a potential friend. His kiss had produced nothing more than a warm sensation against my lips; it certainly hadn't spread that warmth down to my core. Whereas seeing Darius had made my heart almost thud through my chest. I sat for a moment with my head in my hands. Then I pulled myself together, made a flask of instant coffee, pulling a face throughout; and then I grabbed my handbag and set off to work.

Giggles came out of Lucy's office and I could hear Frankie mumbling. What was he doing out in the daytime? It went against his body clock which could make vampires feel really ill. Squeals erupted. Oh for God's sake, what were her and Frankie doing in there? Okay, so it was nothing I'd not done with him myself in my own office in the past but come on. Have some respect for the ex. We'd only been fuck buddies so how did I term myself. Did ex work if you'd not been a girlfriend? Maybe now I was a no-fucks-buddy? I wish I gave no fucks certainly, about anything right now. Whatever was affecting Ebony's mind, I could do with a dose of it.

I wandered through to Shelley's office where I saw her drinking a large coffee with a flushed face.

"Hey, you look better. And you're back on the dark stuff."

She shook her head. "No, it's a glamour." She shook it off to show me a glass of O-neg, then placed it back on. "It was my mum's idea. Don't know how I'd not thought of it. I'm drinking blood but I have it looking and tasting like coffee."

"Now I know why your cheeks are pink. I thought it might have all been down to your randy husband." Shelley's brow creased. "I called you yesterday but Mary said he'd taken you to bed. Had got all caveman about Seth."

"Yes, well the less we talk about last night the better. It was quite eventful."

"Oh? I thought Ebony had come around."

"She did. But then we had to get other people to come around. My mum, Frankie, and Darius."

"What?" I pulled up a chair in front of her desk and sat down leaning closer.

"Well, first, in the throes of passion, I grew fangs and bit my husband."

My jaw dropped.

"Did I hear you right? Did you just say you grew fangs?"

"Yep, fangs. Frankie looked it up, and it's all the baby. But I have to drink loads of blood so that I don't try to take a bite out of anyone else."

I pulled the lapels of my jacket up around my neck. I'd

already suffered random bites in the past, I didn't need my best friend munching on me.

"And then most embarrassing of all..." Her face went red and this time it wasn't to do with her blood intake. "Theo had handcuffed me to the bed."

"Get Theo, going all Christian Grey."

"Yeah, well Theo being Theo, had forgotten the keys to undo them."

"I'm not following. He left them at the shop?"

"Oh no. My loving husband had left them at his best friend's house. He'd borrowed Darius' cuffs... without asking."

My mouth dropped open again.

"Darius had to come free me and do you know how I repaid him? Well you must because he ended up cancelling your date because of it."

I sighed. "No. No I don't."

"Oh. Well I threw up down him. All over his shirt and his jeans. Blood everywhere. We had to launder them while he waited. I'm sorry we messed up you two finally getting together to talk."

"Oh, that's okay." I said, although it couldn't have been further from okay.

I stood up and started backing away towards the door. "Well, it does sound like you had quite the adventure. I'd better get on now. I have a lot to do today.

"Okay, bestie. See you later. Sorry once again for messing up your evening."

I nodded and left.

Back in my own office I almost threw myself down in my seat. Fuck. He'd ended up involved in Theo's mess and then Shelley's vomit. He couldn't make the date because he was stuck at the farm, and what had I done? Had tea with

Seth and then let him kiss me. I was a mess. I was the trollop and whore my father had always said I was. A waste of a person. I'd be better off staying on my own than trying to find a partner.

I'd brave it to the coffee shop just before closing and let Seth know nothing was going to happen between us. At least that was one mess I could get myself out of.

There was a knock and Frankie and Lucy burst into my office.

"Kim, we're engaged!" Lucy yelled excitedly. "I've no ring yet, but I'm going to be Lucy Love. Oh my God, I'm so excited. I must tell Shelley." She ran from the office down the corridor to Shelley's.

"Wow. Congratulations." I told Frankie, who looked more shocked than happy.

"Kim. My actual words to her were supposed to be, 'Babe, can I finger your ring'. But I messed them up and said 'can I ring your finger?'"

"Oh my God. Hahahahahahahahahahaha. Oh thank you for making me smile. Oh my God, hahahahahahha." I creased over.

"Kim, you have to help me."

I tried to catch my breath. "I'm not h-helping you get out of an accidental proposal."

"No." He shook his head vehemently. "I do want to marry her, even though we've only been dating for nine days. I can live with having proposed. She's my one. But I need to do a new one. That can't be it. That's no story to tell our future children."

He took a lingering look at my face. "Oh I can see you're going to be no help whatsoever today. I'm glad my life is so amusing." He went into his jacket pocket and extracted an A4 manilla envelope. "We'll see if your face is still as creased with laughter when you've read this lot. The history of the Withernsea and Hogsthope packs. And thank you, Frankie, for staying up all night. Oh that's okay, Kim. You're welcome."

My face froze.

"Yep, thought as much."

"I'm sorry, Frankie. But I'm having a shit time and that did make me chuckle. I will help you plan an amazing proposal okay? And thanks for this information."

His face relaxed. "Well, I'd better get to bed because I'm starting to feel a bit queasy." He raised a warning finger at me. "Don't you dare say a word about what I just told you."

"I won't. I promise. No woman needs to know her proposal was accidental and if you were going to propose anyway, what's the problem?" Then I launched into Beyoncé's 'Single Ladies' and sang about putting a ring on it. Frankie huffed and zapped away.

I sat at my desk, poured myself a cup of instant and began reading. I took a swig of my drink and winced. It so wasn't what I was used to. This is why you don't shit where you eat, Kim. Leave all the dating agency customers well alone.

I opened the envelope and began reading.

WITHERNSEA AND HOGSTHORPE PACKS - A POTTED HISTORY

(Not to be reproduced. Copyright F. Love, 2018)

Until 1989 the pack was united as one - Withernsea. One member of the pack at that time was Arlo Wild. Arlo was mated with Freya Wild and she was carrying his cub. Arlo had been almost thirty years old when he had mated with Freya.

Arlo became the Alpha of the tribe following the death of his predecessor in battle. Two months before the birth of their son, Darius, Arlo met another wolf shifter from the Hull pack, Renee Thorn. His mating instinct kicked in and he was forced to confess to the pack that he had faked his 'calling' to Freya due to his age and worry about being cast from the pack.

He was thrown out of the pack in disgrace, leaving Freya to care for their newborn son alone. He started the Hogsthorpe pack and declared himself Alpha. Those that sided with him joined him, along with other rogue weres from other packs. The result was that Hogsthorpe has always been a volatile pack, and Arlo ended up ousted as leader and killed in 1992.

Freya Wild had been swept along with the romance and only realised Arlo had not been her true mate when William 'Billy' Phelan joined the pack having moved from Derbyshire. They mated and married and had a further son, Rhett; and daughter, Alyssa. Darius remains a Wild although his mother, stepfather and siblings have the surname of Phelan.

After finding out the above, I sought an audience with Jett Conall, from the Hogsthorpe pack. There he confirmed my suspicions. What follows is for your information only and will not appear in my records.

Jett Conall is ALSO the son of Arlo Wild. His surname was changed in 1992 when his mother remarried.

Jett is Darius' half-brother.

This is the reason the two factions remain so separate. Darius and Jett refuse to acknowledge each other as siblings and their mothers remain bitter enemies. Jett is Alpha of the Hogsthorpe pack, whereas Darius refuses to accept his place as Alpha, instead deferring to Edon Woodland.

Although no clear statement has ever been made, the rumour is that Jett intends to do a hostile takeover of the Withernsea pack and take what he feels is his rightful place as Alpha of the united pack, to honour his father.

There were other words in the text. Stuff about the set-up of both packs and the members but I scanned it, my eyes reading the above words repeatedly.

Oh Christ. And I'd managed to select Jett from the agency's database and call him for a date.

There was no wonder Darius had acted like he had.

I put the document on the table and picked up the envelope to put in the recycling, but noticed another page still inside.

THE MATING OF WERE SHIFTERS - FACTS AND RULES

(Not to be reproduced. Copyright F. Love, 2018)

To ask a wolf on a date is stating your interest in becoming their mate.

To attend the date and eat with a wolf is part one of courtship. Part two is to find out if you are physically compatible through the act of sexual intercourse. Part three is to complete the mating process under the full moon and be bitten by the wolf at which time non pack members become both wolf (if not already) and pack.

Most wolves determine their mate by a scent. This scent is so intoxicating it can lead to periods of overwhelm until mates become accustomed to it.

Should a female show interest in more than one wolf then they must let the female decide. Alternatively they can take out the other wolf.

To cook for a potential mate is a demonstration of the fact you will care for that woman and her future cubs.

When I'd read that, I was ready to throw myself out of the window. I had serious reparation to do. Ebony was right. I really had started a pack war. What if Darius and Jett tried to kill each other now? I needed to do my damnedest to end it. It was just that to do so I would have to confront every demon I had inside me. But I'd do it, for Darius' safety.

My door burst back open and the beaming smile of Lucy greeted me. It was still unnerving seeing an ex-demon happy.

"Many congratulations again, Lucy."

"Oh thank you. But that's not why I'm here."

"Oh?"

"You're one of the reasons I've been hanging around here too. I just had to wait for you to realise that you needed to work on your own demons and then BOOM, here I could be, to let you know I was here to help you."

"You're to help me?"

"Yes. To avoid a pack war and get your man. Are you ready, Kim? I might be an angel now, but it's going to be one hell of a time."

CHAPTER
Eleven

Lucy

I left the office in high spirits. Life was good. I was engaged. I had a fantastic job. Finally, something was going my way.

I heard coins tinkling behind me and pivoted to find Andrew, my predecessor, a few feet behind me. He was supposed to be in heaven having been transferred after almost exposing angels to humanity (not in that way, get your head out of the gutter).

"Andrew? What are you doing here?"

He picked up the coins, putting them back in his pocket and scratched around his neckline. "Oh, I'm back down here, second chances and all that."

"Oh, and have you got a project?"

His face flushed. "Yes, yes, I have, and I need to make sure that this time nothing goes wrong."

I smiled at him. He stepped back a little which I thought was mean. Was my being happy THAT much of a shock to people?

"Well, anything I can do to help, just ask."

"Thanks, Lucy. Well, see you around." He turned and started walking in the other direction. Hmmm, he'd been coming this way before, now he was walking away from me?

Having been one of the devil's top employees, I had a large bullshit-ometer, so I carried on walking for a few minutes and then I turned quickly, fast enough to just see the edge of Andrew's leather jacket disappearing into a shop doorway. I stalked over to where he was pretending to look in the shop window. Unfortunately for him it was a sex shop, and he was currently looking at very large butt plugs.

"So the way I look at it, either way right now you're screwed, Andrew. So what's it to be, fess up, or shall I go purchase the extra-large?"

Andrew sighed deeply. "I'm so going to get fired again. I wasn't supposed to be seen on this job."

My mouth dropped open. "Andrew." I tilted my head at him. "Am I your project?"

"Well, erm, yeah." Another deep sigh escaped him. "So now I suppose you're going to report me?"

"Hell, no." My eyes widened. "If you have an earth angel job to do on me, then get on with it, right now. Save my life or whatever it is you're supposed to be doing."

"I can't tell you what it is, but it's not saving your life. All I can say is that a test is coming."

"Right, I need you to be with me at all times then to get this done. The sooner you're finished, the sooner you can pass your earth angel exam and the sooner I can get back to my life, because..." I beamed again. "I am about to get married."

"Cool." Andrew said, but his face didn't look happy, which made the hairs on my neck stand up.

"Come on, let's go to mine." I told him. "We have a spare room."

Frankie got up a little later than usual due to his having been up in the daytime. He wandered into the living room and saw me sitting beside another man and his eyes flashed red.

"What's going on?"

"Oh, Frankie, darling. Andrew is coming to live with us for a while."

"He's what?" The next moment Andrew was pinned to the wall while a vampire with exposed fangs got up in his business. My fiancé turned to me. "I'm not into sharing."

"Put him down, Frankie. It's not like that. He's an earth angel like me, and apparently he's doing me."

Frankie hissed. "Doing you?"

"As in I'm his project. He's saving me in some way. We're not romantically involved for God's sake. Put the poor man down before he urinates down his own legs."

Frankie dropped him and returned to his usual look and held out a hand to Andrew. "Nice to meet you, pal. Thought about getting a Chinese for tea. You fancy it?"

Andrew went and sat in the furthest corner of the sofa. I heard a clatter at the back door and then a black cat sauntered into the room, walking over to Andrew and jumping up on his knee where she curled up on his lap and started treading his groin area. His surprise at that coupled with an almighty sneeze meant that Maisie was thrown a foot away onto the floor. She landed on her paws, upper back arched, turned around and hissed at him.

I walked over to her with a pet friendly wipe. She hated water but could tolerate a wipe. Then she shifted into her beautiful brunette self.

Andrew's eyes went wide. "You're the cat?"

"I am." She said. "And now I'm wondering how I'm going to inflict punishment on you for throwing me on the floor and coating me in your nose juice. Do you like to be whipped?" She asked him.

"Andrew is an earth angel, Maisie. There'll be no whipping or punishments with him."

She sat at the side of him, far too close, invading his personal space. "Do you earth angels have to be all celibate?"

He swallowed hard. "Well, no, but it's frowned upon if it would distract me from my job and this is my last chance, so all my attention needs to be on Lucy."

Maisie rolled her eyes. "Huh. It's always all about Lucy. Everyone loves Lucy. They even made a stupid TV show about her."

"*I love Lucy* is not about me." I told her.

"She has red hair. You should totally sue the company, they obviously copied you."

"That programme came out in 1951."

"So is it you that's completely unoriginal then? Hah."

Andrew's nose started twitching again.

"I think Andrew here is allergic to cats." I told her, just as she dived across the room, landing on my lap, before another huge sneeze rocked him.

"Ugh. Get off me." I pushed her up.

"Oh well, never mind. I'm in a menage with the couple next door anyway." Maisie smoothed down her hair.

"Being their pet cat is not classed as being part of a menage."

"For an angel you are always so goddamn mean. Cut me some slack here; my love life is seriously lacking, and you bring a hottie here, and he's allergic to me. All-er-gic. And my paws tell me he's packing so I'm really depressed right now." She pouted. "Have you got some of that nice salmon?"

"Oh for heaven's sake. Let me get you some dinner. I'll be back in a moment, gentlemen, please try to not kill each other while I'm gone. I'll fetch you an antihistamine, Andrew, to stop the irritation, although she's following me so it should go off."

Maisie followed me out into the kitchen where I took out some fresh salmon. I put the kettle on ready to poach it, just as she liked it.

"He's hot. It's so not fair."

"Can you behave? He's staying here for a while, hopefully not too long though. Apparently he has an earth angel job to do for me."

"For you? So is shit about to go down in your life?"

"There's no need to look happy about that potential fact."

She leaned against the side. "I'm sorry. You know how it is. When your life is crappy, it hurts even more when you see people getting along with theirs."

I patted her arm, and she started purring and pushing into my hand. It was really off-putting when she did that in human form.

I took my hand away and she eye-rolled. "You're so uptight and missing out. You've seen my tongue, right?" She licked my hand.

"Ewwww."

"Feel how raspy that is? Imagine it there." She nodded at my crotch.

"Maisie. For the umpteenth time, I do not fancy women. I am very happily engaged to a MAN."

Her eyes narrowed, and she hissed. "What's that? I'm sure you just said engaged." She grabbed my recently licked hand. "No ring. Explain yourself."

I put the salmon in a pan of boiling water which distracted her for a few seconds.

"Frankie proposed this morning, in my office. It wasn't

the most romantic of proposals but he did it all the same. We've not had chance to talk about details or a ring or anything yet, because of Andrew." I nodded in the direction of the living room. "So I don't know anything else other than I said yes."

"Can I be a bridesmaid?"

"If you promise to stay in human form. Only I don't fancy untangling cat claws from my wedding dress."

"Lace feels so good in my paws." Maisie went into a daydream. "I used to be able to swing off peoples net curtains when they were in fashion. Now everyone's windows are bare. Bare is in fashion, windows and pussies. It's about time net curtains and rugs were all the rage again."

I was beginning to feel the onset of a tension headache and rubbed at my right temple.

"A few minutes and then your salmon will be ready. So are you happy next door?"

Maisie had popped around there a lot while living with Frankie and they'd taken her in when Frankie was ill (in reality he'd been changing into a vampire). They'd asked if they could keep her as they'd got used to her and Frankie had said yes; but they were human and had no idea that in reality they'd moved a third person into their home. Maisie was under strict instructions not to reveal herself, especially when the husband next door looked like Jason Momoa.

I went into the cupboard and got a couple of antihistamines out and filled a glass with water. "Just wait a second while I take these through." I told her. "Make sure the pan doesn't overboil."

Voices quietened as I got near the room and as I entered I had that feeling that they'd been talking about me. I guessed Andrew might have been instructing my fiance on something earth angel related. I passed Andrew the antihistamines and water.

"Thank you."

"I'll be back in a moment. I'm just feeding Maisie. Would you like a hot drink, Andrew?"

"I'm okay with this water, thanks."

I returned to the kitchen to find an empty pan and an empty room. "That bloody cat." I should have known better to leave a cat unattended in a kitchen with fish. She must have eaten it half-raw.

I threw the pan in the sink and began tiptoeing back towards the living room. Now I know they say eavesdroppers never hear anything good about themselves but well, I did used to be evil, and I wanted to get a heads up about why Andrew was here. I would have to be beyond stealthy as my hubby had vampire super-hearing. I went back and put the radio on in the kitchen. That would interfere with his hearing and put him off long enough for me to get to the room door.

"So what was I saying? That bloody radio. Oh yeah, so basically I've told Kim, that she's to keep it secret because if Lucy finds out, I'm a dead man."

"I'm sure she'd forgive you."

"Forgive me? Are you joking? Can't you tell me what to do to make things right?"

"I can't. I'm here for Lucy, but it sounds like talking it over with Kim was a good idea. You're sure she won't say anything?"

"Lucy would kill her too. It's not cool to deceive a friend like that is it?"

"And Kim's your ex, so that wouldn't go down well either, you two being together like that."

"Exactly. So I don't know what to do right now. I need time to think. To hatch a plan."

I stood in the doorway feeling like I'd been hit by a thunderbolt. What was he saying? Had he cheated on me, with Kim? Is that why the proposal had appeared to come out of nowhere?

I went into the room, both men looking startled. "I'm not feeling so good, so I'm going to go up to bed, okay?"

"Alright, darling. You need anything, just shout down. I'll hear you."

I nodded and went up the stairs to my room. Then I laid on my bed and burst into tears. History was repeating itself. I was losing my man to another woman.

I didn't think I could go through it all again. Look at what had happened last time. Sheer hell.

CHAPTER

Twelve

Darius

"Bro, can you stop thumping around the place? Some of us are studying you know?"

My sister sat at the dining room table, her school books in front of her. I kicked a chair away and sat down on it. "You're a female. Explain something to me."

Alyssa sighed and sat back. "It must be bad if you're actually going to listen to anything I have to say."

I pulled out my tongue. If there was such a thing as a mature male I certainly wasn't feeling it today.

"So the date went well then?"

"There wasn't a date."

"She cancelled?"

"No." I sighed. "I did."

"*Are you out of your freaking mind?*" Alyssa's voice could have been heard in Australia. "Is this something to do with the emergency you rushed out on?"

"Yes, it meant I had to cancel."

"Oh well, that couldn't be helped, just rearrange."

"I went to see her at her house—after I'd dealt with the emergency—and well..."

"Spit it out, brother."

"I saw her with another man. They kissed."

She was out of her seat. "The bitch. I will go kick her arse."

"Alyssa, sit down."

"Do you want me to drag her here by the hair? I can do that you know. They've accidentally left that paragraph in the Shifter Handbook."

I rubbed a hand over my brow. "No, Alyssa. I want you to sit down and shut up for a moment so I can TALK. TO. YOU."

"Spoilsport." She flopped back down into her chair. "Okay, I'm listening."

"This was a different male. Not the shifter scum, but a human who works at the coffee shop. I don't know why she's doing this. Our connection. It was strong. She's my mate, I know it."

"Have you heard anything from the mutt?"

"No. If he sets foot near here, or near her, I will tear him limb from limb."

Alyssa sighed. "Look, Darius. Have you tried talking to her? She's a human, she probably doesn't understand any of this."

"I want to talk to her but I need her to ask me out again. They are the rules. She has to do the instigating. I can't see it happening. Especially if she's started dating one of her own kind."

"Look, Darius. Do you want her, or are you prepared to let one of the other two have her? The way I see it, it's like she's playing a real life version of that Marry, Date, or Dump, and right now you are definitely the dump, a turd. So it's time for action, man."

I ran a hand through my hair; it cascaded down around me.

"Come on." Alyssa got up.

"Where are we going?"

"For a haircut. Time to ditch the stereotypical werewolf look. I don't think she wants to date Fabio."

"Oh no! You look like Liam Hemsworth. Now I can never watch Hunger Games for sexual stimulation again. You spoiled Liam for me for life." Alyssa mock-shuddered. "But in terms of a lady-boner, Kim's will be raging when she sees you."

"What did you get up to last night anyway, until I got home?" I couldn't stop feeling at my head. It felt like a tennis ball. Around my neck was cold without the hair covering it. I'd kept my stubble though. No way was I going clean shaven.

"Here, give her this Hunger Games boxset when you see her. I no longer need it." Alyssa's swift subject change was not lost on me.

"Alyssa..."

"Oh calm down. I went to the cinema with Sophie. Now anyway," she walked over to me and smoothed down the grey chambray shirt she'd insisted I change into along with some denim jeans. "Now, are you ready to get up from the dump?"

"Yeah, I will be."

"Will is no good. Oh and is Kim a brunette? Slim, tall?"

"Yeah, why?"

"Because there's a livid looking woman walking up to our front door, and that's what she looks like." Alyssa gathered her books up from the table. "I'll be upstairs, supposedly studying, but probably eavesdropping, so don't go at it in here will you? Sterile food surfaces and all that."

I walked up to the door and opened it just as a fist was about to rain down on it heavily; so instead Kim punched my chest. Her hand lingered there a moment as if she was temporarily frozen. We looked at each other and that whole staring thing happened again. Eventually the staring competition broke.

"Your hair..."

"Yeah, I've had it cut."

"It looks..." She shook her head. "We need to talk, Darius Wild, and I'm not leaving until you've listened to me."

A smirk danced on my lips. "You'd better come in then."

Kim walked in and looked around. "Nice place. Yours?"

I shook my head. "My parents. I'll get my own place when I marry. My wife gets to choose."

"Oh." Silence permeated the atmosphere. This shit was awkward.

The door flew open and Alyssa stomped through. "Oh, I didn't realise we had visitors. Sorry." She held out a hand. "I'm Alyssa, Darius' younger sister, and you are?"

"Kim. Kim Fletcher."

"Oooh, you're the Kim he never shuts up about."

I was going to kill her.

Kim's eyes went wide. "Well, err."

Alyssa wrapped her in a hug. "Oh, no hand shaking for you when you're practically family. Well, let me just get a quick glass of water. I'm studying you see. Upstairs. Been there for hours and so got thirsty." She filled a glass with water. "Darius, you offered Kim anything yet? A drink. FOOD."

Kim's face went bright pink. Then Alyssa was gone as fast as she appeared.

"I must apologise about my sister. She's a teenager. I think that explains everything."

Kim smiled.

"Anyway, come through to the lounge and take a seat. I'll make you a coffee, seeing as I know how you like it, and would you like something to go with it, like a pancake?"

"A pancake? Like you're going to cook one for me? Do you not have something easier like a biscuit?"

"I have but I was just about to make pancakes." I lied.

"Erm, okay then, I'll have a pancake. Thank you."

She couldn't possibly know what me cooking this for her meant, could she? Or did she? If she did, she'd just accepted it.

WHOA.

"Right, I'll just be a couple of minutes."

"I'll wait with you in the kitchen, if that's okay? We can talk."

Oh God, now I was understanding why men trembled when women said they wanted to talk.

I started preparing the pancake mixture. Kim hovered nearby.

"Last night, Darius..."

My hand tightened around the whisk.

"I'd just gone for a drink with Seth. I thought it was as friends. He took me by surprise when he kissed me. It was one-sided. I don't feel that way about him. Actually, I popped into the coffee shop after work yesterday and made that clear."

I turned to her. "You did?"

"Yeah. My, erm, earth, erm, friend, suggested I come and speak to you. She says we keep dancing around each other and getting nowhere. I'm sorry, Darius. I'm sorry about arranging the date with Jett. I'm sorry about last night's misunderstanding. This is really hard for me..."

It was really hard for me too if you get what I'm saying...

I dropped the whisk, grabbed Kim's shoulders and pushed her back against the kitchen wall. My mouth crashed down on hers hungrily. I'd imagined this moment for a long time and the reality was so much more than I could have anticipated. I pushed her thighs apart with my knee, grinding my erection against her heat. We devoured each other, moans and groans coming from both of us.

A loud banging noise came from upstairs and we sprung apart.

"Sister right above." Alyssa's voice yelled.

We both stared at each other and then collapsed into laughter.

"Bloody siblings." I told her. "Right, where were we...? Ah, yes, pancakes."

We sat opposite each other at the dining room table and I watched as she tucked into her pancakes. Food... that I'd cooked for her. My indication I would care for her and our future offspring.

"I've been reading up on were shifter culture and traditions." Kim said slowly.

"Oh?" I swallowed.

"I'm aware that by asking Jett out I inadvertently put myself up as a potential mate for him. Although as a human I think that sucks. Surely if I don't know this stuff, it can't count?"

"We can't force you, but we can still fight amongst ourselves for the opportunity."

"I know who he is to you, Darius."

Time stood still. Of all the things I was waiting for her to say, that was not one of them.

"He is no one."

"He's your half-brother and your enemy. I wouldn't call that nothing."

"Sounds like you really have done your homework. So what else have you learned?"

"That I need to ask you out on a date to put you on an equal footing. So I'm going to ask you again. Will you come out with me, tonight? I'd better say 9pm now I'm being filled with pancakes."

It wasn't the only thing I wanted to fill her with. Alyssa was a cockblocker.

"Do you know what the step after that is?" I asked her slowly and carefully.

Her cheeks flushed again. "Yes, I do. Darius. I don't do... well, I haven't done relationships. Now, I know it sounds cliche, but I had family shit and it messed with my head. I find it hard to trust people, to let myself go. But I want to try, Darius. I want to try, with you."

"Okay." I smiled. "Nine pm tonight it is."

She finished her pancakes and leaned closer. "Bring a toothbrush just in case," she whispered.

Then she got up and walked to the door. I wanted to pick her up, put her over my shoulder, and take her to bed. But I had to be patient. For all her bravado it looked like actually my mate-to-be scared easily.

She turned toward me at the door and reached up on her tiptoes, brushing her lips across mine.

"Oh and Darius...?"

"Yeah?"

"Thanks for the pancakes. But I already could tell you were the sort of man who'd care and provide for his family." She smiled and walked down the path. "Nine pm, and if my annoying friend or her husband ring you, tell them you're the one tied up tonight." She winked.

I closed the door and leaned back against it. My head resting on the glass inset.

She knew.

CHAPTER Thirteen

Kim

Oh my fucking God. I had a date with Darius in a few hours and there was a pretty good chance we were going to get it on afterwards. Stripped of my clothes I headed to the shower. I needed to make sure everything was shaved and moisturised. Just the thought of seeing him again had my stomach in knots. I wasn't sure I was actually going to be able to eat anything. Crikey, I'd better change the bedding and do a bit of housework. I looked around at the mess. I needed a miracle. Then I thought of one.

I dialled Frankie's number.

"Hello?"

"You know that problem I'm helping you with?"

"Yes...?"

"I'll make it super spectacular if you can zip over here right now to do me a favour. It won't take you long, but it's an emergency."

He sighed down the line. "Just a second."

The doorbell rang and sure enough Frankie was standing there, his hair a little mussed from the speed. "This had better be good. I had to make an excuse to Lucy because we had dinner reservations."

I handed him a bottle of furniture polish and a duster.

"You know your super whizzy speed?" I said, and I displayed my best begging expression.

Fifteen minutes later the house was immaculate thanks to my super slow vacuuming and Frankie's super fast everything else.

Frankie stood in the doorway, ready to zap off again. He nodded at my towel turban and robe. "You might want to get dressed then for your date."

"On it now. Thank you so much, Frankie, you're a star." I kissed him on the cheek.

"Yes, well my proposal better be the more epic for all this." He told me.

"It will. I'll get my thinking cap on. Have a nice night with Lucy." I said.

"God, yes." As he looked at his watch, his cell phone rang out. He took it out of his pocket.

"I'll be right there." He said and then he was gone.

I kept it smart casual and wore jeans and a red silky v-neck. I walked into Hanif's to be greeted by Rav, who worked there. Rav was a demon.

"Hey, Rav."

"Come in. Welcome to Hanif's. We are very happy to be assisting in this most auspicious occasion." He escorted me over to the man himself who stood up.

"Take your seat, Darius. I have it, my friend." Rav pulled my seat out and gestured for me to sit down.

"Rav, I've eaten in here loads of times and you've never pulled my seat out for me, what's got into you?"

"This is a special occasion, Kim. You are out on a date with one of my closest friends. Now, excuse me while I go and get you complementary poppadoms and a pickle tray." He raced off.

I looked at my date. Darius had changed into a black tee and jeans. I couldn't stop staring at his arms. They were so muscled and defined. I'd bet he could pick me up with just one.

"I would have liked to have pulled the seat out for you myself, but it would seem my friend is determined to make our date special." A smirk flirted on Darius' lips.

"Thank you, but I'm perfectly capable of sitting down. It's one thing that has me a little uncomfortable about the whole wolf thing. You're like 'I will feed you, take care of you, pull out your chair'. I've been on my own a long time. I can take care of myself."

"You can but you shouldn't have to. Sometimes it's okay to let someone else take over for a while. Just imagine it, you get in from work and I have a bath running for you. You climb in and the heat soaks away the stresses of the day. Then while you do that I'm cooking dinner. You come down, eat, and then I make love to you all night long. Are you telling me you have a problem with that?" He raised an eyebrow.

I'd lost my words, lost them completely at 'make love to you all night long'. I'd felt that beast against me when we kissed. The thought of it inside me, well... NO. WORDS.

So it was as well that Rav came over at that moment with the poppadoms and pickles because at least eating gave me an excuse for not talking for a while.

"I am so happy for you both, that you finally made it here on a date. My friend has been wanting to date you for a very long time." Rav stood beside us and smiled.

Darius' eyes flashed yellow, and it made me gasp. It was a reminder that not only was he a man, he was also a wolf. A goddamn animal.

"Thanks, Rav. If you could leave me and my date alone now for a while it would be appreciated."

"Oh, yes. Sorry. I will go make sure your starters are being prepared."

I laughed. "A long time, huh?"

"Well, I'd seen you around, but once Theo started to date Shelley, you were even more on my mind. But you were dating someone else, so that was that."

"Me and Frankie weren't dating. We were just..." *Fuck buddies.* I couldn't say that to Darius. "Friends."

"I know what you were. I have to accept that you have a past, that we both have a past. But let's concentrate on the future, shall we?"

"Yeah." I looked into Darius' eyes. I felt lost and found at the same time. Something was most definitely happening between us. I felt like I'd known him forever. It was hard to describe, but I just felt sure I'd found the one. Oh my God, what was happening to me? I'd been hit by the lovey-dovey train.

"Erm, have you finished, only you've been sat staring at each other for seven minutes now?"

"Oh." I sat back. "Yes, thank you, Rav. I'm ready for my starter."

He rushed off with our plates and I looked at Darius and giggled. "We keep doing that."

He nodded. "It's because you were meant for me, Kim." He held out a hand towards mine.

"Kim!" A voice shouted out breaking our connection.

I turned around to find a certain barista standing behind me. *For the love of God. Not now!*

"Seth? What are you doing here?"

"I thought I'd grab a takeaway but seeing as you're here I might just stay and eat. I'm not interrupting anything am I?" He began to pull out a chair.

"Seth!" Lucy rushed towards us. Where the fuck had she come from? "You can eat with me and Frankie if you're feeling lonely. Over there." She pointed to a far corner of the restaurant while wearing a look that said don't even try to refuse me.

Seth's face fell. "Sure, that would be lovely, Lucy." He stared at us. "Well, have a nice evening."

He walked over to where Frankie was settling into a seat. I saw Frankie's brow crease, and he looked over at me with a confused look on his face. Staring back at him, I shrugged my shoulders.

"I'm only doing this because it's part of my earth angel duties. I'm watching you, Fletcher." Lucy spat out, before stalking off to her table.

Not knowing what the heck had just happened, I looked at Darius. His eyes were yellow, and he was growling.

"Oh, shit. You're not going to change here are you? In the middle of the restaurant?"

Darius leapt from his seat and ran out of the door.

I got up to follow him.

Seth stood up. "Have you been ditched? I'd be more than happy to take over as your date." He yelled.

"Sit down!" Lucy commanded.

By this time the other restaurant customers were watching the event like it was match point at Wimbledon.

I didn't know what was going off with Seth and Lucy but right now all I could think about was Darius. I threw some money on the table and took off after my date.

Standing at the doorway, I couldn't see him anywhere. He must have changed and taken off. If I was him then I'd have headed for the pack's woodland. I ordered a taxi and headed for the caravan park.

I knocked on the door of his home and Alyssa answered.

"Oh God. You're supposed to be on a date and yet you're here and Darius isn't. What went wrong this time?"

"I think he changed into his wolf so I'm guessing he's out there." I gestured towards the woods.

"You see the woods?"

"Yeah, why?"

"They're glamoured."

I shrugged my shoulders. "Not to me."

"Huh. Well, come on." She grabbed her coat. "I'll take you. We need to make sure that he's there and that there are no other wolves out there, don't want you eaten up, do we?"

I followed her into the woods and she called for her brother. After a few minutes there was movement at the edge of the woods though it was difficult to see what was happening as it was part shaded by trees.

Then my mouth fell open. There stood a huge wolf, with golden blonde fur and yellow eyes. That was Darius in wolf form?

"I got it from here." I told her.

"You sure?"

"Yeah."

Alyssa moved away as I moved forwards.

The wolf bowed its head as I moved nearer. "Darius. Stay still. I want to see you." As I moved closer, my heart thudded in my chest because it was a fucking wolf. I hoped to God he wasn't about to eat me seeing as he'd only had a couple of poppadoms. I got closer. Now what did I do?

Carefully I reached out and touched the wolf's fur. It was soft and felt lovely to my fingers. I began to stroke and pet the wolf, and he laid down on the grass. I sat next to him and snuggled close, carrying on stroking his fur. "You make a beautiful wolf, Darius Wild, but any chance of you changing back into a guy? Only it's getting cold out here and I'm really hungry."

The wolf shivered, and I watched as Darius appeared on the ground. A completely naked Darius. My eyes looked over every single inch of his body before resting on his now very erect cock.

"Oh my." I said.

"Still hungry?" He growled.

"Only to be filled with meat." I replied, and he grabbed me and carried me further into the woodland.

He took me to an area where there was a yurt and after checking that no one else was inside, he carried me in and laid me on a bed where he covered me in blankets. Then he headed towards the centre and lit a fire.

"I'm sorry our date got cut short. But I saw Seth, and then your ex, and it was too much. My wolf wanted to claim you. I had to get out and change."

"Your wolf is magnificent." I said. "Although you have to appreciate it's hard for me to get my head around the fact you are part-beast."

He sat beside me on the bed. "You would be too. You know that don't you? If you decide to become my mate. I will bite you and you will change."

I sat quietly. It was a lot to take in. When thinking of the future and marriage and babies you thought about changing your second name, not your DNA.

"Well, first before we worry about all that, don't we have to check we're compatible?" I stared at the handsome man sat beside me, and then I leaned over to him and raised my head next to his so I was staring up into his eyes. I brushed my mouth against his. A growl erupted deep in his throat and then he claimed my lips with his and I forgot all about the cold.

There was no slow tease, this was a fast dance. Darius took off my shoes, discarding them on the floor, and then his hands were at the waistband of my jeans, where he opened the button and lowered the zipper before pulling them off my legs. I lifted my arms so he could lift my top up over my head and then I was left in only my mint green lacy bra and matching panties—for about three seconds before they were also removed and thrown to the floor. Goose bumps rose on my skin with the nip in the air, but then I was covered by a well muscled and warm body and all was okay in the world.

I could feel his cock, hard against my thigh, and my core went slick at the thought that soon he was going to be inside me. Darius nuzzled at my neck before grazing his teeth down over my breasts, capturing my nipples in turn and giving them a gentle nip.

I shivered, but it was with anticipation, not cold.

He pulled covers up around us and whispered in my ear. "Next time, I'll take my time, but right now. I can't."

His cock teased at my entrance and then he pushed inside and we both groaned with pleasure.

He filled me to the hilt and then drew back and pushed again. My hands gravitated to his buttocks, and I felt them clench with his movements. I wrapped my legs around him drawing him deeper inside.

"Fuck, you fit me perfectly." He whispered in my ear and then he took my mouth with his.

His kiss was almost brutal. He claimed my mouth as he claimed my body and I felt myself climbing the dizzy heights to orgasm, and then I exploded, taking Darius over with me. We were panting, it had been so, well, animalistic.

He gathered me in his arms. Darius was so broad that I felt like a waif in his arms. For a moment I tensed, feeling vulnerable, and then I thought fuck it. I was warm, cosy, and well fucked. Why was I trying to ruin this for myself? It was okay to give in to my feelings and they were telling me to lie in this man's arms feeling protected.

We had dozed, but then I awoke, feeling fingers teasing between my legs.

"This time I'm going to take my time with you. Until you're at my mercy and begging for more."

My heart rate quickened in excitement.

Sure enough, a few hours later one thing was for certain. We'd passed the compatibility test with flying colours.

CHAPTER

Fourteen

Lucy

Earlier that evening...

I didn't know what to say to my fiance after overhearing his conversation with Andrew last night. He'd only just woken anyway, so I decided I'd save my questions for later. We were going out for a meal and I didn't want to ruin date night. Except the phone rang and his eyes got a shifty look about them. Information for those dating ex-demons—betrayal can be spotted a mile off.

"I've got to pop out." He told me.

"Oh yeah, where?"

"Bloody Kim. Apparently she's got some kind of emergency. There's always something with that lot: Kim, Theo, Shelley. Do you think we'll ever get a quiet night on our own?"

I folded my arms across my chest. "So don't go."

He tilted his head at me. "It's an emergency. I won't be long."

"Well, I'll come with you."

He shook his head. "You get ready and go get our table at the restaurant. I'll meet you straight there."

Then he stood up, kissed my cheek and whizzed off.

I needed to follow him. Only my wings were so

goddamn fluffy and enormous he'd spot me if I tried to fly, so I'd just have to get a taxi. Luckily the angel realm held an account with A1 Cabs. Angel 1 to those in the know.

I was just about to climb into the car when I felt something hard poking me in the back, something I'd not experienced for a day or two. I turned to see Andrew having premature wingulation.

"Put them away." I scolded.

He managed to get them to disappear.

"Look it's your fault, my angel bleep went off. Now I don't know what you are doing but I have to strongly advise you against it."

"I'm only going to have a nosy at what my fiance is doing." I gave Kim's address to the taxi driver.

"Can you hold on a minute?" Andrew said. The cab driver shook his head in agreement. "Take as long as you like, my meter's ticking. Always drama with you Angels. By the way, quick question. Any of you have a boss called Charlie?" He let his head roll back and cackled with mirth. It was times like this I wish I'd still got my pronged fork.

I turned to Andrew and tried to smile sweetly. "If you stop the cab setting off again your mission will fail because I'm going to push you out of it, which evil doing will no doubt get me benched by Team Angel. So, sit there, watch me and I figure as long as you don't let me kill Frankie, we're good. I can't promise though."

He sat back and sighed. "I'd better get my job after this because they gave me the hardest gig ever."

We pulled up down the road from Kim's and I made the cab driver put us in invisible mode, one of the perks of Angel Cabs. So we all watched as Kim's door opened and Frankie stood there on the step. She stood on the doorstep in only a robe and with a towel on her head, freshly showered, and then she leaned over and kissed him on the cheek.

My hand was on the door handle of the car, but Andrew leaned over and with strength I didn't know he possessed he moved my hand back to my side and very bluntly said, "No."

I flashed him a look of hurt and anger.

"I'm your earth angel. You must be guided by me right now. No, Lucy. This is not the right path."

The fight left me and I leaned back in the cab, my head against the back of the leather seat and I fought back tears. "Surely he wouldn't do this? And Kim, I thought she was wanting to date Darius. I can't believe them."

"Can you take us to Hanif's Indian Restaurant now?" Andrew asked the driver and once again we were on our way.

On route I got a text from Frankie telling me he now needed to go to see Theo again as he had a query about Ebony.

Was that the truth or had he turned back around for another round with Kim?

"Actually, I'd like to detour to The Marine." I told our driver. "I think I need a few mojitos."

It was an hour later when I got a call from my fiance saying he was at the restaurant and where was I? Andrew helped me walk from the bar to the restaurant entrance as I was a teeny bit wobbly on my feet due to lack of food and three cocktails. We were just about to cross the road toward Hanif's when I saw Seth dart into there. Then there was a bleep from my bag. My angel bleep had sounded. Seth was about to do something stupid.

Andrew recognised the sound. "Him?" He nodded toward the restaurant entrance.

"Yes." He picked me up and ran with me across the road, through the entrance and down the stairs.

I ran over to my project. "Seth." I shouted, hearing him say he'd sit with Darius and Kim. On their date? Mind you, she did seem to be creating her own harem at the moment. Seth shot around facing me, his face masked with disappointment. "You can eat with me and Frankie if you're feeling lonely. Over there." I pointed to where Frankie was sitting, looking at me in confusion.

"Sure, that would be lovely, Lucy." He replied though his face said anything but.

"I'm only doing this because it's part of my earth angel duties. I'm watching you, Fletcher." I spat out, before stalking off to my table.

"Lucy. Is this, or is this not date night? Only you've arrived with two other men." My boyfriend said.

"If I were you right now I'd be quiet." I told him, my jaw clenching.

"Have you been drinking?" He sniffed near me. Stupid vampires and their enhanced senses. "Mojitos? You went for mojitos? With him?" His fangs descended. It was laughable. I'd just followed him to another woman's house, and he was acting like I'd done something wrong when he knew Andrew was my earth angel.

I was about to speak but then I heard a growl from across the tables. Darius' eyes had turned yellow, and he looked like he was about to shift. He bolted out of the restaurant. Surely, she'd not confessed about her dalliance with Frankie, had she?

Seth stood up. "Have you been ditched? I'd be more than happy to take over as your date."

"Sit down!" I commanded.

Kim took one look at me, shrugged her shoulders and then throwing money from her bag onto the table she ran out of the restaurant.

"Are you ready to order?" Rav said.

"No." Four people spat out at him at the same time.

Rav took a step back. "Whoa, you do know I'm the evil one right?" He said. "I'll give you five minutes."

"So where have you been?" I said to Frankie.

Andrew's pager went off. Bleep. Bleep. Bleep. In other words, shut up Lucy.

"I must go see that Kim is okay." Seth said. Bleep. Bleep. Bleep. My pager went off.

Rav came over. "Can you turn those off? They are the same bleeping noise as the ovens. We keep thinking food is ready when it is not."

"We can't, sorry, Rav."

"Well, are you ready to order now?"

"No." We all said again.

So I wasn't allowed to ask Frankie where he'd been. Great. Well as it happened, Seth was looking like he was ready to bolt so my mind was currently occupied as to what the heck was going off with him.

"Seth?"

"Yeah?"

"What's going on? You are acting very strangely."

He sat back in his seat. "I don't want her with that Darius guy. He's not for her."

Frankie turned to him. "I'm sorry, dude, but I really think he is. It was prophesied you know. Ebony, before she lost her visions, she saw it."

"I refuse to believe it. I believe in another outcome."

"Look, you have a crush. I understand. Kim's an attractive woman. I went there myself in the past."

Andrew shot up in his seat.

"You're making my job very difficult for me right now, Mr Love. Maybe you could please think before you speak, you know, in front of your fiancée."

Frankie looked perplexed. "But she knows my past. I know hers. I just saw her ex-boyfriend down at Shelley's. We all have a past."

"You saw Dylan?"

"Yes, everyone is trying to see what they can do to help Ebony."

"Is she in a bad way?" I asked.

"No, quite the opposite. She's loving not having any visions and wants to go on a holiday. We're trying to explain that seers can't have breaks from their visions. That it's not normal. In the meantime I'm trying to consult with Margret on whether we can think of a spell to help when they do return. Shelley is not so well with the pregnancy tonight, hence Theo called me over to help."

Theo was calling my current boyfriend to help my ex-boyfriend's wife—the one who stole my previous boyfriend. I think I'd be having words with Theo at some point.

"Lucy, love?" He meant it as a term of endearment but I heard it as my to be married name.

"Yeah?"

"Can we go home and I'll make you and Andrew an omelette? I've lost my appetite and I think this date night is a bust."

I had to agree.

Frankie whizzed home to make a start on supper while we got another angel cab. We dropped Seth off at his apartment. He exited the car without saying goodbye and walked up the street with his shoulders slumped. I guessed unrequited love could do that to a guy.

The taxi set back off and Andrew turned to me. "Thank you for listening to me. I cannot stop your actions. I can only advise as you know."

I searched his face for answers but there were none to be found. "Yes, I do know, and that's the only reason my fiancé didn't find his face tandoori'd tonight. Because I finally have faith. It took me a long time to find it, but you are my earth angel and if you are advising me to not pursue this, despite what it looks like, then I'm listening. I want you to get your wings properly, Andrew, and I also want to believe that I'm not seeing what I appear to be seeing."

He nodded. "Thank you."

"But if I'm wrong and you've fucked up again, I'll skewer you and make you an angel kebab." I told him. He shot a few feet away from me. You could lead an ex-demon to the good side but you couldn't always make her drink—unless of course it was a mojito.

CHAPTER
Fifteen

Kim

I woke wrapped in blankets and Darius. It was heavenly until my stomach decided to let us both know that I hadn't eaten properly since the pancakes and the poppadoms.

Darius' head shot straight up. "Oh that won't do at all. I can't have my woman hungry."

My woman. Those words should have scared me half to death and had me running out of here, but instead they made me break out into a big beaming smile. *What was happening to me?*

He leapt out of bed and I let my eyes wander down over his muscled back, over those thick legs, and that taut ass, as he bent to pick up my clothing from the floor. Okay I could have done without that last visual. Next time avert thy gaze as he bends right over, Kim, but the rest of it *oh my.*

He insisted on dressing me, which took another hour, seeing as he insisted on kissing my skin over and over as he placed each clothing item on my body. Then he got a fresh robe from a cupboard in the yurt.

"We're well stocked because as I'm sure you can imagine, we tend to lose our clothes a lot."

"It's like you're the incredible hulk but not green." I laughed.

"Oh I get green all right, especially when I think you're kissing other men."

"I'm not kissing any other men."

He walked over to the bed and scooped me up in his arms. "Damn straight." He said. "Now I'm going to take you back to mine and get you some breakfast."

He held me in one arm as he used his other hand to push the door open. So he could do it. How strong was he? He put me down, and I turned around to see that on this occasion the kitchen was full.

"Meet the family." Darius said, completely unflustered by the fact that he was in a robe. Luckily there was an outbuilding behind the yurt that had a small bathroom so I'd been able to wash myself a little and remove as much of yesterday's makeup as I could without my face wipes.

"Come take a seat." Alyssa said, a huge knowing grin on her face. "I bet you're starving both of you. Big night?"

"We went out for an Indian." I said quickly. "And decided to stay in the yurt so as not to disturb you as we were late back."

Darius laughed, a great hearty guffaw.

"Darlin', family of wolves. They can smell our coitus. No good being embarrassed around here. Now take a seat and let me get you a large breakfast, because yes," he looked at Alyssa and winked. "We have a huge appetite this morning. So, I'll let Alyssa introduce you to everyone because I can see she's dying to do so." He patted me on the butt before pulling out a chair for me at the table.

I sat down at the table with my head in my hands. I'd never been so embarrassed in all my life. Staring at the table,

I daren't look up because I just knew there would be several sets of eyes looking at me.

Then the smell of coffee appeared under my nose and I decided it was worth the stares to be able to drink this much needed nectar of the gods.

I clutched my hands around the mug and took a sip even though it burned my tongue.

Alyssa waved her hand around. "Okay, so, Kim. This is our mum, Freya; dad, Billy; and my older brother Rhett."

They all smiled at me.

"It's a pleasure to meet you at last, Kim." His mum said. "I know your journey here has been a little tricky." There was an underlying tension in her words. This mama was protecting her cub.

"Yeah. I'm sorry. I didn't understand pack rules and I know I've made a mistake that can have ramifications for the pack. If there's anything I can do to undo the mess, well, just let me know. In the meantime I'm reading up on pack rules so I don't do anything else that's stupid."

Darius served me a huge plateful of bacon and eggs before his mother spoke again.

"Well, if you mate with my son on the next full moon, there will be no war with Hogsthorpe as there would be no point. Darius could take on his true role as Alpha of the pack and they would be of no threat."

"Mother." Darius scolded. "We've had one date. One. Please leave any further dating and mating stuff for me to discuss."

"You've slept with her, and Jett hasn't." His mother stated clearly. "So once that news reaches the mutt's ears, which it undoubtedly will, Kim will be in danger, as he'll want to even the score."

I dropped my fork. "You mean he might..."

"Attack you? He's not allowed via pack rules to do that but he could just to spite Darius. However, he could use coercion, threaten other people to make you do his bidding. So the full moon is next Friday and I suggest we make an announcement as soon as possible."

I slammed my fist onto the table. "This is my life you're talking about. I get you have beef with Jett and his mother. What Darius' father did to you was unforgiveable, but I've been on one date with your son. You can't expect me to commit the rest of my life to him after one date." I leaped up from the table and then I did what I always do when faced with difficult situations. I ran.

Heading past the rows of caravans I ran until I'd left the park. A bus was coming and I jumped on it, letting it take me to Withernsea centre. I didn't feel like going home as I expected Darius would turn up there. I really did need to eat now. I was starting to feel faint with the lack of food because I had expended a LOT of energy the night before. It was my day off, and I'd thought after eating I would spend the rest of the day with Darius, getting to know him better—both his body and his mind—but no, here I was again all by myself.

I realised I'd walked up to work. Oh sod my day off, I needed to keep occupied. I unlocked and headed up the back stairs to find myself flung up against the stairwell wall tied in blue webs.

"Oh, it's you." My bestie let me back down gently, her eyes changing from a weird blue back to normal.

"What the fuck, Shelley?"

"Kim, when have you ever, EVER, come into work

unless you were rostered? So forgive me if I thought we were being broken into."

"You have me there I suppose." I pouted.

"Anyway, what are you doing here?"

I climbed up the rest of the stairs. "Do you think I could actually get past the stairs and then I might tell you."

I followed her into her office and took a seat. "I'm sorry to disturb you at work but I didn't want to go straight home."

"What's wrong?" Shelley walked up to me and placed a hand on my arm.

"It's Darius."

"Oh, what's happened now?"

"It's the pressure. I didn't know I'd set off this pack war thing. Then I find out Jett is Darius' half-brother, and now his mother wants me to mate him on the next full moon in a week's time!"

"Steady on there, rewind. Jett is what? Whose mother? Or is Jett's mother also Darius' mother? I'm lost."

I went through everything bringing my best friend up to date.

"Flipping eck, Kim, you don't half know how to fuck up spectacularly."

"I know. So now what do I do about it?"

"As the current head of Withernsea, I'm going to ask for a meeting with Edon and Jett. They are the alphas of the pack. I need to discuss the situation and ask for it to be taken into account that you are not pack, and were not aware of pack rules and therefore events should be excluded, unless you commit to them with full knowledge."

"You'd do that?"

"I would think it's part of my duties. Even though you are my best friend, you are also a Withernsea resident and you are being held hostage to mate with a were shifter in order to avoid the repercussions from another shifter. I think in this day and age we should be able to choose our own partner, not be tricked into it or forced into it by arcane rules."

Shelley took out a bottle of blood, drank it down, and then followed it straight with another.

I sat there with my mouth agog.

She wiped her mouth. "As you can see, my thirst is getting worse. Theo and I are proposing that I go to the Caves soon to be turned. I have an appointment there tomorrow for assessment. That's one of the things I was doing here today, seeing if I could get through what I need to do in case I can't make it into work next week."

"Tell me what I can do to help." I said. "I could do with my mind taking off things."

We worked steadily all afternoon. Shelley had brought in a hamper full of food that Theo had supplied and insisted she take with her to satisfy any hunger she had so I had had plenty to eat. I was ready for a coffee from Jax's though, so I decided that before I went home, I'd treat myself and get a coffee and a doughnut.

"Thanks for everything this afternoon, Kim. I'm hoping to be in this week but it depends what they say at the Caves tomorrow."

"Well, keep me posted. I worry about you, you know? My best friend, the half-wyvern/half-witch, soon to be mixed with vampire. When I first met you at that dating event, I didn't realise what a weirdo I was getting involved with."

Shelley laughed. "There's a way to go before we get as weird as some of that lot! Anyway, you can talk. You might yet become part-wolf."

"I really do like Darius, you know?" I told her. "But I don't like being rushed into things. This is potentially my first serious relationship. I can't cope with the pressure. I just can't."

"There shouldn't be any pressure. Leave it with me. If I end up being turned then my dad can step back in and help sort everything out. He'd probably love that, lording it over the wolves."

Me and my bestie hugged each other.

"Take care of you and that baby first and foremost. I'll manage to get myself out of the mess I'm in. It's not like I haven't had practice."

I said goodbye and made my way down to Jax's.

The best thing about a close friend running a coffee shop was that even if the sign outside said closed you could knock on the door and be let in, and if there was anything left in the baked goods section you got them for free.

Seth let me in.

"Hey, Seth. Where's Jax?"

"I'm in the back, babes. Knee deep in invoices." A voice shouted out.

"Can I get a coffee to go, Seth, please?"

"Sure thing."

"Pack her a selection of cookies and cake, Seth, if you don't mind."

"Has she been this bossy with you all day?" I asked.

"Worse." Seth winked. We both knew Jax was lovely. "Sit down, I'll bring everything over."

I waited until my coffee was prepared and a cardboard box filled with treats. Seth walked over to the table and hovered.

"Kim, I need to apologise for my behaviour last night. I'd had a bit to drink, and well, I got a little jealous seeing you with Darius. I'm really ashamed of myself now. Don't worry, I totally get you have me in the 'friend zone'."

"No worries, Seth."

"Look, on Monday, can you get me some dates organised? I need to get myself back out there. Truth is, you remind me of my ex-wife, and I guess I'm still not fully over her. Maybe if I have some dates with other people, I can finally move on."

"I'll get you all sorted. Thanks for apologising, but there's no need. We all do stupid things when we've had a few too many. Any idea why Lucy was being weird with me?"

"Lucy's weird with everyone isn't she? She keeps telling me she's my guardian angel and sometimes follows me around."

"Well that's true enough." I took a taste of my delicious coffee and then I stood and picked up that and my bag of goodies. "Ah, bliss. Tonight it's just going to be me and my coffee and cake."

Seth stood up. "It's time for me to leave too. You not seeing Darius tonight then?"

"No." I didn't elaborate. It was none of his business.

"I'm off, Jax." Seth yelled.

Jax came out front. "Sorry, I'm being rude. I'll catch you Monday, Kim. First coffee on the house because of my lack of manners. Seth, thanks once again for everything. See you Monday too."

Seth saluted her then turned to me. "Right, seeing as I pass your house to get to mine, do you want a lift?"

"Yeah, that would be great. If you don't mind." I was tired after all my late night shenanigans. Maybe the coffee would wake me enough to cook a pizza.

I sat in Seth's BMW and sunk into the seat. After

having a nice big taste of it, I placed my coffee in the drink holder and put my bag of goodies on the back seat. God this was so much better than catching the bus. After a minute I felt my bum becoming warm and felt at the seat beneath me.

"Heated seats." Seth laughed.

"Jesus, Seth, I thought my arse had gone into the menopause."

The heat soaked into my back too and as the events of the evening took their toll. I closed my eyes.

When I woke up I did that 'where am I?' thing for a minute and then I remembered I was in Seth's car. I turned to him. "Shit, sorry. I didn't mean to fall asleep. How long was I out?"

But while I asked the question I was staring out of the window trying to get my groggy, confused mind to work out where I was because it wasn't at my house. I could feel sleep trying to pull me back under.

"What's happening? Where are we, Seth? Just take me home will you?"

"Sorry, Kim. I'm afraid I owed a debt and delivering you was my payment. You'll wake up soon. I only put a small dose of sedative in your coffee."

"Wh- what are you talking about?"

My passenger car door opened, and I turned and looked into the face of Jett Conall.

"Well, hello there, Kim. You'll have to forgive the way I got you here but I couldn't see you coming willingly. Now the sedative is going to have made you all kinds of weak, so me and Seth here are going to help you into the building."

My eyes went wide.

"I can promise you I've not brought you here to harm you. Just to talk to you. But please don't try anything silly because I'd hate to have to change my stance on violence towards women." Jett smiled but rather than create warmth it chilled me to the bone.

"What do you want? Just take me home, Jett. This is stupid."

"I'm only taking you home once we've had a little chat. And as for stupid. Well the only one of us being stupid here was you *when you slept with my brother.*" He spat the word brother out like it pained him to say it. "Now he's in front and I don't like that, Kim. I don't like that in our current challenge he is winning."

"He's not winning. I'm not a chess piece, ready to knock over, you know. I'm a human being."

"Yes, you are." He said. "So utterly human, but not for long, hey, Kim? Because soon you will be my wife, and a wolf."

My mouth dropped open, but he held up a hand before I could speak.

"I suggest you keep that pretty mouth quiet for now, while we get you inside. Otherwise just like that chess piece you spoke of, I will knock you over." He made a fist of his hand, leaving even a half-awake me under no illusion as to what he meant.

"So are you coming quietly?" He said.

I nodded and undid my seatbelt.

I was in so much trouble.

CHAPTER

Sixteen

Kim

As I tried to get out the car, I looked at my surroundings. We were in an Industrial estate. I tried to find the name of it but all I saw from that moment on was Seth's butt as he carried me over his shoulder and into one of the buildings. Inside I was taken into an office area where my bag and phone were taken away from me before I was lowered onto a ratty old sofa. I was starting to come around and did my best to glare at Seth and Jett. Seth sat at my side obviously to stop me should I attempt to get up, and Jett carried a chair in front of me. I watched as he sat himself down, a smug smile on his face.

"Kidnap. Really, Jett? You can't get dates the old-fashioned way now, you have to have us bundled into cars?"

"Actually you got in the car willingly." Seth said.

"To be given a lift home!" I yelled. "Now take me back."

"You're not going anywhere right now, Kim, so you might as well get comfy."

I gave Jett the side-eye. "I'm telling you now, and you." I glared at Seth, "you came between me and my coffee and I don't know when, but at some point you will both pay."

Jett guffawed. "Oh you're going to make a brilliant wife. I'll need to hone that temper so it's only in the bedroom though. I shall look forward to our fireworks."

"If I get my way, I shall stick a roman candle right up your arse, and then I'll give away wolf kebabs to anyone passing."

Jett threw a scarf at Seth. "Tie her mouth with that will you? It's time for her to start listening."

I shot up from the sofa but Seth was a lot stronger than me and between him and Jett my hands were tied behind my back with one scarf and then another was fastened around my head and over my mouth.

I was pushed back onto the sofa. I could feel my wrists already going dead with the tightness of the scarf and I tried to move the one across my mouth by moving my lips but it was no use.

Finally I sat still and subdued. My heart thudded as I realised I was now powerless and in a warehouse with two strong burly men.

"Mmmm. I smell your fear. Good, maybe now we can get somewhere. So, now I have you compliant in front of me, let me explain what is going to happen. Firstly, I am going to cook for you and you will eat it and enjoy it. I have to demonstrate my ability to care for you and our cubs and although my wife is the one who will be in the kitchen, barefoot and pregnant, I will follow the rules to be equal to my enemy."

I could still glare at him so I did my best evil eye.

"And you will be pregnant. Continually. Because it is my intention to breed a whole new Conall clan. My sons will be strong and will rule Withernsea."

I wanted to say that Shelley would never stand for that, but I still had the stupid scarves on. It was becoming plainer to me that Jett was almost feral. Whereas Darius was a man with an element of wolf; with Jett it was almost the reverse. His wolf ruled him. He barely seemed human at all.

"Now, Seth very kindly let me know that he overheard that your dear best friend, Shelley, is pregnant. Pregnant with the forthcoming ruler of Withernsea and well, I shall want to make sure my clan work very well alongside her child. So to that end this is what is going to happen, Kim. You will be released from here, later, when I feel like letting you go and feel I can trust you, and you will tell everyone that you are rejecting Darius and that on the full moon this following Friday you shall become my wife. I shall prepare the announcement and the ceremony. If you fail to do this, I will make sure everyone knows about Shelley's secret pregnancy and I will raise a bounty on her head so that she's too busy fending off death threats to help you."

My eyes went wide.

"Oh good, it looks like this is being understood."

He was insane. I tried to stand up but Seth just pushed me back down. Tears of frustration began to roll down my face.

"Look, she's so deliriously happy, she's crying." Jett laughed.

Jett was a stunning looking man with his hazel eyes and dark hair, and yet while he basked in his victory plans he looked cruel and it gave an ugliness to his appearance.

"So, here's what's going to happen. We will leave you here for a while to get used to the fact you're at my mercy, and then I'm going to make you something to eat, and I suggest you eat it all up like a good girl, because I don't think you'll like the consequences if you don't. Now I'm not into rape, I just want what is mine fair and square and so even though I can smell that dog has had his hands all over you and sullied you with his seed, I will be the bigger person and let you go home, once you've accepted our

135

engagement. After we mate at the full moon, you will become mine anyway once I've bitten you."

He stretched his arms above his head. "So that's what's going to happen, unless of course you start trying to play silly buggers, and I really suggest you don't." He tilted his head at me. "Because my bounty-on-Shelley's-head post is ready to be sent. I just have to press the button."

He laughed at me.

"Okay, Seth. Let's leave her in here." He looked at his watch. "It's eight pm now. I'll come back in the morning at eight am. See how amenable to my plan she is after twelve hours of no food or drink. You sit in the security office and watch her on the monitor from there. Don't go in, she's a clever lady. She'll try to get free."

And with that he walked out of the room. Seth following behind him. The door slammed, plunging me into total darkness and that was me stuck.

I laid back on the sofa for a moment trying not to let the panic seep into me. The last thing I needed to do was have a panic attack or for me to attempt something stupid and fall and hurt myself. As my eyes became accustomed to the darkness, I looked around the room, seeing if there was anything I could use to get my hands free. If Seth caught me, then of course I would have to face him but I had to try. I got myself off the sofa and walked around to the edge of the desk and backed my wrists and the material against the corner and tried to rub through it, but it didn't work.

I guessed that Seth was watching me, probably laughing at my vain attempts to get free. Eventually I gave up and went back to the sofa. I'd just have to try to sleep away the hours until they came to me again. I was cold, hungry, and knew at some point I would need to pee. The saddest thing of all was that I didn't know when anyone would actually realise I was missing. I mean would they? Shelley had said see you Monday and her mind was on her appointment with the Caves. Same with Jax, she wouldn't know until Monday if I failed to turn up. Darius might try to contact me, I suppose, but it couldn't be taken for granted. My family certainly wouldn't care. That was one thing about a pack. A big group like that, they looked out for each other. I bet they'd notice if someone went missing.

And then I cried.

I cried for the family I didn't have.

The love I'd been too scared to embrace.

The predicament I was in because Jett had me held hostage and not only physically.

Until I knew Shelley and her baby could be safe, I would have no choice but to follow his instructions. I just had to hope to God that in the meantime I thought of something to help us both.

It was a long and uncomfortable night, spent with only my thoughts to keep me company. As the door opened and light came in, I winced while my eyes got accustomed to the brightness.

"Take the mask off her mouth. Leave the one on her wrists for now." Jett commanded Seth.

I stayed still while he undid it.

"Hmmm, you're not looking so feisty today, Kim. Have you thought about my proposal?"

"I have." It came out as a croak. I was so thirsty.

"Take her to the bathroom, and get her some water while you're there." Jett commanded. Seth dragged me up and along the corridor to a bathroom. The odour of urine hit me as soon as I walked in. A typical men's urinal.

"Can you help me?" I said. "I can't get my pants down with my hands being tied."

It was the utmost in humiliation and I would never forgive them for this. I'd had the devil himself tried to kill me and it hadn't hurt me this bad.

As Seth helped me pull my pants back up I brought my knee up and smacked him in the mouth with it. He backed away wincing with pain. My knee was in agony but it had felt good to inflict pain on him.

He wiped his mouth, a touch of blood coming away from a cut on his lip. "I guess I deserve that. I'm sorry. You're not the only person he's blackmailing. If I could help you, I would."

I wondered what he'd done to Seth, that would make him assist in a kidnapping. It must be pretty bad. But regardless I was here directly because Seth had brought me, so there was no sympathy coming from me whatsoever. I despised him.

Lowering my head under the tap that Seth put on, I took several large gulps of the water. I'd never take simple things like that for granted again.

Then I was taken back to the office.

"Oh, Kim. I hope you didn't try to escape."

"No. Just an accident." Seth said, "while I tried to assist her in the bathroom."

"You can untie her hands now. They'll take a while to get the strength back in them anyway."

When the scarf was untied I rubbed my wrists against my body frantically. I was in so much pain from how long they'd been tied.

"Okay here's a slice of toast I've made you. Eat that and then I've fulfilled my feeding part of things."

He thrust the toast into my hands and I was so hungry I ate it too fast. The bread felt like it was stuck in my throat.

"Right, so let's conclude our business shall we? So all I need from you now is your signature on this piece of paper that says you agree to marry me on Friday night and mate with me under the full moon. As soon as I have that signature I can send out the engagement notice and the invitations. The woods at the back of this industrial estate are lovely for the ceremony and then for the evening reception I think we'll go take over our rightful land in Withernsea."

He placed a pen on the desk. "Soon as you sign that, you're free to go." He laughed. "Well, obviously you're not free. I mean you've a wedding outfit to sort out. Make sure the undies are nice won't you? Oh, and do you like home movies, only I was thinking of filming us and sending my brother a copy. Then again he'll probably be dead and not able to watch it."

"Please don't kill him." I choked out. "I want to save my friend and please leave Darius. If you take the pack and me, is that not enough? If he's alive he'll suffer more watching us, won't he?"

Jett scratched his chin. "You have a point. I can't let him live long because he'll try to find a way to retaliate, but maybe just for a little while I could let him watch me gloat."

I walked over to the table and signed the paper. It was official. I was engaged to Jett Conall. Our wedding set for Friday evening. I had just over five days to pray for a miracle.

Seth dropped me at home. Come Monday morning he would be back at the coffee shop as normal and I wasn't allowed to say a word. The minute he suspected anything, Shelley and her baby's life was in danger.

I had to go back to being Kim, the selfish bitch, and I didn't like it one bit as it had taken me until now to realise I'd finally lost her.

CHAPTER
Seventeen

Lucy

I sat in the office typing up Frankie's latest findings on supernaturals. My angel bleeps had developed malfunctions, going off over and over again, driving me mad. When I'd called Seth to check he was okay and asked him if he'd seen Kim he'd told me that they were out together having dinner and her phone battery had gone flat. Everything was okay, so why did I have a feeling in the pit of my stomach that things weren't okay at all?

Frankie had been his sweet usual self. I don't know what his secret was and how Kim was involved but I was 90% convinced now that they weren't having an affair. Not completely because he had left her house while she was wrapped in a bathrobe, but she'd not snogged him on the doorstep which I would have done if someone had just boned me good and proper. I was doing as advised by Andrew and waiting it out.

Theo had called first thing saying that the Caves had decided to admit Shelley for turning after she'd bitten him again last night. I'd assured him that Kim and I could cover. All we needed now was for the lady herself to turn up.

The door to her office banged. Talk of the devil. I went in to tell her about Shelley.

"Fuck, you been on the lash all weekend?" I said as I

141

took in her haggard appearance. She had dark bags under her eyes, like she'd not slept for a month.

"Yeah, I've been celebrating." She said.

"Celebrating?"

"Yeah. I'm engaged, just like you. No ring yet though, we're going to get that later."

"You, and... Darius?"

She shook her head.

"Seth?"

Her head shook again.

"Not my Frankie!" I screamed.

She cut me a look. "Don't be ridiculous. I'm engaged to Jett. Jett Conall."

"Who?"

She actually eye-rolled me. "Jett. He's a were from the Hogsthorpe Pack. I was on a date with him the night you first got together with Frankie."

"Oh, him. And you're engaged. Already? How long have you been dating?"

"Three days. I mean when you know, you know, right?"

"So when's the wedding?"

"Friday."

"Friday?" I yelled. "This coming Friday?"

"Yeah, so as you can imagine I have lots to do, to prepare for married life. Sorry that I'm taking the edge off your proposal a little by getting married first."

"Does Darius know about this?"

"No, what business of his is it?"

I held my hands up outstretched. "None, unless you consider that four days ago you were out on a date with him."

She waved a hand at me. "He's of no consequence. Now I'd better go see Shelley and see if she can help me shop."

"Oh, Shelley's at the Caves. We've to cover for her. She'll not be out until Thursday morning apparently. She bit Theo again and so she's being turned."

"Oh that's good. Until Thursday you say?"

I furrowed my brow. "It's good? That your friend is being turned into a vampire?"

"She's married to one and having a baby one, well a mix up with vamp in it, so it makes sense for her to be one. I'll be part-wolf on Friday."

I smacked myself in the forehead. "Have you taken some hallucinogens? Actually, have I taken some hallucinogens?"

"I don't know. Have you?"

"Well, you tell me, because I'm sure you've told me that you're marrying a werewolf on Friday, one that I wasn't aware you were dating; plus you're happy, rather than worried that your friend is in the process of being changed into a vampire."

"Just a regular Monday morning really working here." Kim said nonchalantly. "Anyway, I'm hungry and thirsty so why don't you pop down to Jax's and get us both a coffee and some cake? Seeing as Shelley is off I reckon that right now that makes me your boss, right?"

The old me would have singed her hair off. The new me smiled and agreed. Mainly because something was wrong—very, very wrong. I'd get our drinks and question Seth, see if he could shed any light on the problem.

I'd returned to my office to get my bag and purse when an almighty white light almost blinded me. I turned around to find my boss, Angel Sophia, standing in front of me, looking all celestial in a long white dress covered in diamante.

"Oh, thank goodness you're here. My pagers aren't working properly." I told her.

She walked over and gazed down into my eyes. "Lucy. Your pagers are working perfectly. That's the amount of trouble both your charges were in, and you ignored them."

I gaped at her. "But..."

"It's not your fault. We're looking at an alternative communication system. This one was poorly thought out. It's really hard to get everyone on board with technological advances though when most of us are thousands of years old." She sighed. "Anyway, Lucy, your main challenges have arrived. Both of your charges have made or are going to make mistakes that could have repercussions for the whole of Withernsea. It's time for you to step up, Lucy. You're needed. The angels above need you to take care of the potential hell about to be wreaked down here.

"I knew it. I knew there was something off about Kim's wedding. Leave it with me, Sophia." I said. "I got this. I promise."

"I hope so." She said and then with a kindly stroke of my shoulder she disappeared in a blast of white light leaving only a trail of white feathers behind her.

Definitely the first thing I needed to do was talk to Seth. I needed some help though to get to the bottom of things. I could no longer be evil... but that didn't mean someone else couldn't.

The coffee shop was packed with people once again. This was getting on my nerves now. Damn, I didn't want to wait in a long queue and I needed to talk to Seth. I decided that seeing as it was being done with good intentions it would be okay and so I shouted FIRE at the top of my voice until everyone had run out screaming.

I'd run through to the back just in time to stop Jax from actually calling the Fire Brigade. "Sorry, Jax. I needed to talk to Seth urgently."

"So you created panic in my customers and cleared them all from the shop? It had better be life or death, Lucy. Life or death."

I'd never seen little Jax with attitude before. It was actually kind of amusing though inappropriate, you know, on the lines of a circus freak show. *Let's watch the angry pixie squeak.* Yeah, I know she wasn't a pixie. I'd already had an encounter with a real one of those, but she was short, okay?

"I'll get them all back in afterwards. They'll just be admiring all the little doggies in the grooming parlour. It's all bitches on heat around here these days."

Jax rolled her eyes and went out the back. "Shout me if you need me, Seth."

"Everything okay, Lucy?" He asked me.

"Yeah. Just needed a coffee for me and my friend, Kim. And two chocolate doughnuts. Only we're busy today. Shelley's off."

"Oh? Everything okay?"

"Yeah, fine. Well, it is with Shelley. Listen, you were out with Kim on Friday night, right? That's what you said when I called you. Only she's in a mood today. Not talking much."

"Yeah, we had dinner."

I nodded my head. "Thought so."

"What?"

"Well, she was with Darius Thursday night, and you Friday night, but after that she was with yet another man and well, I hope I don't upset you telling you this, but... she's marrying him."

"She is? She's getting married after having been out with me Friday night? That's disgusting." Seth pulled a face. "Well, that's just charming that is."

"I knew she wouldn't have told you. She's so blase. She used to date my fiance you know. I'm surprised she's not in the tabloids with her exploits—the *I have a different guy every day of the week* stories. I think I should find this Jett dude and have a word with him. Let him know what she's like. It's not fair. She's probably given him a disease." I stared. "You didn't sleep with her did you? She's probably riddled."

"No. No. Listen, I would just leave her to it. She must love the guy if she agreed to marry him."

"Well, she loved him yesterday, but today's Monday, maybe today it's the postman's turn or something. I think he deserves to know what he's getting himself into."

"Seriously, I wouldn't. I once tried interfering in someone's business and well, it didn't end well for me." Seth said, his head dipping down.

"Oh look at that. I'm letting our coffees go cold." I said. "Okay, I'll keep my mouth shut. It's her life after all. I'll just concentrate on my own wedding."

He nodded.

"Right, I'll just go apologise to Jax again and then I'll go out the back entrance and up to ours, so thanks, Seth, and I'll see you again soon."

"Yeah, see you, Lucy."

I walked into Jax's.

"Sorry about that, Jax. Listen, you know how busy you are? Did that start the same day Seth started?"

"Yeah. Aren't women fickle? Get some man candy and they're here like a shot."

That word hit me like the cold jet from a water pistol.

Shot! Could that be it? Was there something in the drinks? Things weren't adding up where Seth was concerned.

"Yes, unfortunately we are. Yet if a guy did that to us, we'd call them a sexist pig. Good to be a woman, hey? Well, I'll see you soon."

I went back out to the cafe. "Sorry, Seth. I can't find my mobile. Just seeing if I left it out here. Oh there it is." I said, lifting it out from behind the napkin dispenser. "Oh, do you have a tray I can borrow for carrying this stuff? It's burning my hand a little."

As he bent down to get a tray, I switched my drink with one left by a human customer.

"Thanks, Seth. I'll stop being a pain now and get out of your hair."

The moment I returned to my office, I quickly dropped a coffee and bun off with Kim and then I sat at my desk and pressed play on the phone. I'd left the voice recorder going while I'd gone into Jax's.

"Jett. It's Seth. Listen, if you get contacted by a woman called Lucy, as far as she's concerned Kim was with me all Friday night, all right? No. No, she's not suspicious. She's fine. No. There's no problem here. I've got it covered. Just promise me please that when you're in charge of the pack, you'll get her back for me. That was what we agreed. You'd get the pack, and I'd get my wife back. Yeah, man. Just tell me when to drop the news and I'll do it. Withernsea Gazette. On it. Okay, Boss. Yeah, jobs secure, can keep a close eye on her from here. That love spell is working like a charm. A charm, get it? Oh yeah, bye then."

I listened to it one more time and then I knew I had a wait ahead of me. Until my vampire fiancé would be out of bed and could help me make sense of all this and what could be happening. I carefully picked up the drink I'd took from the coffee shop and put it in the small space behind the filing cabinet. I couldn't afford for it to get tidied away.

CHAPTER Eighteen

Darius

We'd been called into an urgent pack meeting, so I made my way quickly to the Hall. I walked in to find everyone being handed a sheet of paper. The way they looked at me when they read it filled me with dread. Edon passed me a copy. It was a printout of an email sent to the pack.

To: Withernseashifters@btinternet.co.uk
From: Hogsthorpeshifters@btinternet.co.uk
Date: Monday 5 February 2018
Time: 07:00
ANNOUNCEMENT

The Hogsthorpe Shifters are delighted to announce the engagement of Alpha Jett Conall to Kimberly Louise Fletcher on Friday 9 February 2018 at 9pm.
The ceremony will take place in Hogsthorpe Hall before the newlyweds consummate the wedding under the full moon in Hogsthorpe Woods.
Hogsthorpe pack only in attendance.

End of message.

I fell onto the nearest seat. "What? This can't possibly be right. She wouldn't do this, so he's forcing her somehow. What do we do? What can we do?"

Edon looked at me in a kindly, fatherly way. "That is why I have called the meeting, Darius. I know how I would proceed but on this occasion I feel you should direct the pack.

I sat for a moment with my hands steepled, my elbows resting on my knees. Trying my best to breathe slowly through my nose and quiet the wolf threatening to erupt from me to rip out Jett Conall's throat.

"Okay. I feel I need to see if Kim is with Jett or at home. If she is at work, I shall attempt to talk to her as a first course of action. We shall reconvene at midday once I have more information.

Edon nodded and the rest of the pack murmured their agreement. With the next meeting set, the others left, leaving me with Edon.

"Spoken like a true Alpha." Edon smiled. "It would seem when it comes to discussions about your mate, you find your confidence."

I considered what he was saying.

"She makes me feel whole. If she marries that mutt, I don't know how I'll survive."

Mates were our everything, and I had no doubt in my mind that she was mine.

He nodded, and I left, grabbed my things and set off on my bike to drive to Kim's office.

~

I walked to the back door and knocked with such force that I put several dints in the door. A buzzer sounded and Lucy's voice came out.

"Darius. Pack it in, or I'm not letting you in. And straight to my office, not Kim's, we need to talk first. You got me?"

"I need to see her," I growled.

"Won't do you any good, and I have intel so you need to speak to me first. Comprendez?"

I sighed. "Yes, okay. You first."

She sounded the buzzer and ignoring her instructions I stomped straight into Kim's office.

Kim startled when I walked in.

I held up the piece of paper. "What's this shit about you marrying Jett?"

She looked me straight in the eye, no smile on her face, just a dead-eyed look. "What about it?"

"Don't give me that." I roared. "What's he doing? It's got to be blackmail because no way would you marry him voluntarily."

She stood up. "Not true. I intended to marry him all along."

"Then what was all the other night? Sleeping with me, meeting my family? I know you felt what I did."

At this point the door flew open and Lucy stood there. "God, you stubborn arsed manbeast."

"I didn't feel that, Darius. I just pretended, so as to crush you further. That was my plan all along and well, look at you, it would appear I'm succeeding."

"This is bullshit." I punched the wall with my fist. The plaster broke off in chunks and dust rained down on the floor.

I turned to Lucy. "Sorry, I will have that made good." I

moved back around to face Kim. "Stop your lying and tell me the truth. I can help you. The pack will help you."

"The truth is, Darius, that I love him. He's my true mate and I'll be marrying him on Friday. You need to deal with it."

She sat back down on her chair and started tapping on her keyboard.

"That's all you're saying?"

"Yes, to be honest I'm bored now, and as I'm sure you can imagine, with my wedding being on Friday I have a lot to do, so if that's all... unless you want me to put you back on the dating agency books now with you being a free agent?"

I stomped out of the office, Lucy moving ahead of me and then I swung the door shut with such force that I ripped it off its hinges.

"I'll be back, shortly." I said to Lucy and then I ran down the stairs and behind some storage sheds where I sat down and calmed my breathing so I wouldn't change because if I did I was going to be out of control.

I'd smelled her when I'd walked in. My mate. MINE.

The words she'd said. I couldn't believe that they were true because if they were... well it didn't bear thinking about. I needed to throw down against Jett.

"What you thinking there, looking all Beast?"

I looked at my hands and felt around my chin. Fur. Oh shit.

"Lucy. I'm sorry."

"Sorry for not coming to my office and listening to me? Well, better we get to talk here actually. Out in the fresh air and away from Kim." She took a seat on a concrete step at the side of me. "I think she's being blackmailed by Jett, and Seth is involved somehow. I overheard him on the phone. He said something about Jett getting him his wife back.

I stood up, flexing and stretching my arms. "So I need to talk to Seth."

"No. And I insist this time, Darius. No bull in a china shop. I'm waiting for Frankie to wake up because there's something else going on. The coffee is being spiked. That's why there are so many customers. I want Frankie's expertise on everything before we decided on a course of action."

"What's Shelley said about this? Surely she thinks it's crazy what her friend is doing?"

"Shelley's in hospital being turned right now. Theo's with her. So she can't help."

I thrust out my chest. "Right, I need to get back to my pack for midday to make plans. I think I shall make a challenge for supremacy."

"Look. Could you change your meeting time to say, 5pm? Then I can attend and bring Frankie. Only I know you have pack business, but like I said this goes deeper than that. I've been given a job to protect Kim, Seth, and Shelley, so I need to know what your plans are. Seriously. Don't take on the angelic realm."

A white feather floated down in front of my eyes at that point.

"See, there's your message. Don't piss us about."

"Okay." I exhaled. "Five pm at the caravan park. Ask for the meeting with Edon on reception and they'll show you through."

"Thank you. Please in the meantime don't do anything stupid. Not until I'm up to date with everything. I need Frankie's files on the packs so that I'm up to speed."

"Lucy, I can tell you anything you want to know right now. I suppose we should start with the fact that Jett is my half-brother."

Lucy groaned. "Oh this just gets better and better."

"The meeting has been re-convened at 5pm. In attendance today it is our honour to host Lucy Fir and Frankie Love. To those who are unaware: Lucy is an ex-demon and is now an earth angel with the current responsibilities of caring for the futures of Kim, Shelley Landry and a Seth Whittaker, a barista from Jax's whom we shall discuss in due course. Frankie is an ex-wizard, now vampire, who is researching supernatural history." Edon stopped speaking for a moment and the pack welcomed Lucy and Frankie. "I would now like to invite Lucy to speak."

"Thank you, Edon." Lucy said, extremely respectfully and politely. "I have known Kim Fletcher for quite some time now, and it is my opinion that she very much cares for Darius here, even if she's too stupid to admit it. There is obviously something else going on, blackmail or whatever, that is forcing her to carry on with this wedding charade. Since she first met Jett at the restaurant, she has made no effort to see him since, and only called him to apologise for involving him in a bid to make Darius jealous. However she was only able to leave an answering machine message."

"She recorded this information on her non-interest in Mr Conall?" Edon clarified.

"Yes, your honour, I mean, Edon."

A few shifters laughed only to be silenced by a glare so evil it could only come from someone who'd spent time in hell.

"Darius, as a Police Officer in special investigations, could you manage to trace this message?"

"Possibly, I could get someone to do it."

Edon nodded. "It is evidence that can help us."

Lucy continued. "Now, the Barista, Seth. He has for

some reason been placing a love potion in certain coffees. Not all, but enough that Jax's has had a steady stream of customers over the last few weeks. I'm not sure in what way this ties in with everything but I need to find out. Also Ebony, Withernsea's Seer, has been without her visions for the last few days. This also needs investigation."

Edon looked over to me. "Would you like to direct the pack or shall I?"

I cleared my throat. "Alpha Edon, I would like to suggest the following as a possible course of action. Firstly, we reply to the Hogsthorpe email with our protest and challenge."

"What does that mean?" Lucy interrupted.

"That we do not accept the engagement notice, as one of our pack wishes to challenge for the position of mate. This in pack law is a declaration of war as Darius would be directly challenging Hogsthorpe's Alpha. Something I suspect is exactly what young Master Conall wanted, as if he wins Darius he can then directly challenge me as Alpha, and potentially take over the whole pack."

"That's what Ebony saw." Lucy said. "It's coming true."

"After this, I propose we capture Seth Whittaker and bring him here for questioning. Holding him here until after our business with Hogsthorpe is concluded, or until the marriage of Jett and Kim has taken place should it still proceed."

"I agree." Lucy said. "We need to find out what's going on. Although if he goes out of contact it will tip Jett off that something's not quite right."

"Jett knows exactly what's happening." I told her. "We've no time to lose." I turned to our secretary. "Please prepare the protest."

To: Hogsthorpeshifters@btinternet.co.uk
From: Withernseashifters@btinternet.co.uk
Date: Monday 5 February 2018
Time: 18:00

STATEMENT OF PROTEST

In accordance with the Shifter Handbook please take note of Chapter 4, Section 2a.

We hereby declare a protest with regards to the forthcoming marriage of:

JETT CONALL and KIMBERLY LOUISE FLETCHER

Please note receipt of this statement and choose a time and place for this matter to be debated.

ALPHA EDON WOODLAND

End of message.

With the protest sent, it was time to bring Seth in for questioning. We agreed that we would await the response from Jett and that nothing more should be done today. Lucy and Frankie went home, and I went back to my family where I had the great task of letting my mum and my sister know that we were about to go to war.

To: Withernseashifters@btinternet.co.uk
From: Hogsthorpeshifters@btinternet.co.uk
Date: Tuesday 6 February 2018
Time: 07:00

ACKNOWLEDGEMENT OF PROTEST

In accordance with the Shifter Handbook, Chapter 4, Section 2b. A meeting has been arranged for:

Thursday 8 February 2018, 7pm
Building One, Henry Smith Retail Park
Herring Road, Hogsthorpe.

End of message.

CHAPTER

Nineteen

Kim

I could barely motivate myself to get dressed. In fact, it was only the fact I was covering for Shelley that made me get out of bed to shower and get ready for work. Seeing Darius yesterday had almost killed me. Since we'd slept together there was a pull drawing me to him. Keeping my distance was physically and mentally hurting me. I couldn't explain it beyond it being some kind of physiological or biological response.

I was also worrying about Shelley. Was the turning going okay? Was the baby alright? There had been no word and no response to texts although reception at the Caves could be funky.

The truth was, I had nothing to do for the wedding now. Jett was arranging everything. Obviously he didn't trust me. He'd called last night reiterating his threats and telling me to spend the next couple of nights packing my things because Thursday evening I was to gather my essentials and move to Hogsthorpe. My other belongings would be collected after the wedding. I hated what was happening to me, to my life. Maybe I only had to stay married to him until Shelley had the baby? It was going to rule Withernsea. Surely she could take it from there? Yeah, I just had to wait out the birth. But by then what would have happened to me? What would Jett have done to me? Would the mating itself make me like him? Love him even? Would he have killed Darius or at least reduced his pack to such a position that he would hate me? Passing my hall mirror I stared at myself. Where was the girl with the attitude who stood up to her father and didn't stand for this crap? She just wasn't here today. Too many bad memories flooding my mind.

There was a knock at the door. Sighing, I walked over and looked through the spyhole.

Alyssa. Darius' sister.

Fuck.

"I know you're there. I can smell you. Open the fucking door. We need to talk."

I walked away and wandered back into the living room to sit on the sofa. I couldn't risk being seen letting Alyssa in. Hopefully she'd go away.

There was an almighty cracking noise, and I cowered behind the sofa. The next thing I knew I was being pulled out by the roots of my hair.

I whimpered in pain, following her where she walked to keep my hair in my scalp. "I've come to see what the hell you're playing at. My brother just declared war. War. For you." She pushed me onto the sofa.

"W-what?" I gasped.

"News of your engagement was sent by email. He, well, the pack on his behalf, replied. They refuse to accept the ceremony as official and so a meeting has been arranged for Thursday evening. He's keeping it close to the wire is Jett. So what I want to know is do you love Jett or Darius? And don't give me any shit because as you can see I deal it, I don't take it."

I stared at the growing woman in front of me. No fear

and full of sass, she was everything I was a few weeks and months ago. I burst into tears.

"Such a mess. Such a mess." I shook my head.

Alyssa looked around. "Ah. Just a sec." She went out of the room and came back with some toilet tissue and a paper and pen. On the paper she wrote:

In case you're being bugged.

I scrawled on the pad.

He threatened to kill Shelley and the baby. I can't risk that. Not even for your family. Shelley's baby is the future ruler of Withernsea. She has to come first, above us all.

I gave her the pen back. She nodded and wrote on the paper.

Do you love my brother? If you had a choice, would you choose him?

I took the pen back.

With all my heart.

I'm sorry for pulling your hair and shouting.

It's okay. I guess if I had a sibling I'd do the same.

Sorry about your door. I'll get it fixed.

God, what was it with these wolves and doors?

In case we're being recorded I need to say some more shit and then stamp out. Carry on as normal and know that we have your back. We will sort this and we will make sure your friend and baby are okay.

Listen, if it comes to Shelley and the baby, or me. You choose <u>them</u>, you promise? I'm expendable. They aren't.

My brother wouldn't agree, but I promise.

Alyssa stood up. "Right, now you're a little more subdued, stay away from my brother, you hear me? He deserves better than you. You're a tramp, going after all those men at once. Jett deserves you. Come near us again and I'll hand you your arse." She winked at me and then left.

Her words, although a joke, should have stung, coming as they did on the anniversary of my father's death. It was a reminder of all the things he'd used to say to me. But I wasn't a tramp. I had to remember that. Blowing my nose again, I went into the bathroom and splashed my face with cold water and then I brushed my teeth.

Where are you Kim? I said in my mind to my reflection in the mirror.

I'd said myself in my writing that I was expendable at the side of Shelley, and without a life with her and Darius in it, what was the point? There was no point in anything if my future was a life with Jett.

So what did I have to lose? I may as well come out fighting. I'd look for the cues coming from the Withernsea pack and I'd look for a weapon. Anything I could use to take Jett out.

It had taken a young girl to show me the way. Her attitude reminded me a lot of myself at that age. Standing up for myself against my father. He hadn't changed me, and neither would Jett.

I was ready to fight.

CHAPTER

Twenty

Darius

I looked at the paper my sister gave me and I couldn't believe my eyes.

"Oh my God. I don't know whether to kill you for going to see her alone, or hug you for what's written here."

"Can you do neither, cos I like my life and then there's my personal space."

"So that's why she's marrying him. Can you see, she would give up her life for the ruler of Withernsea. She is such a suitable mate."

"Yeah, whatever, bro. Maybe instead of dreaming, you could formulate a plan that takes care of the heir, ya know."

"Seth is being picked up as we speak. He frequents a gym that has a handy back entrance."

"Yeah, well any trouble and I'd go for *his* handy back entrance, with a sharp stick. Now, it's been swell chatting with you, but I have things to do."

"Please take extra care, Lys. Especially right now. I don't want a Hogsthorpe mutt near you."

But she just waved me off as she headed out of the door.

No one put my baby sister in the corner.

~

Seth's eyes were wide as he sat on a chair in front of the pack. Some of whom had turned into their animals for added effect. His hands were bound behind him and his feet were tied to the chair.

Once again Edon had stood back to let me proceed.

I paced in front of Seth. "So, I'll just let you listen to this." I played the message Lucy had recorded and his face fell. He couldn't deny what was so blatantly there. His head hung.

"My ex. She went off with one of his pack. I went to see them. He promised me he'd get her to come back if I helped him. All I did was watch Kim, man. I didn't harm her. I just had to try to disrupt the two of you getting together. Try to get her to date me instead until nearer the full moon."

"What was the deal with the love potion in the coffee, and how did you choose who got it?"

"Everyone got it. It just works on some people and not others. I needed to make sure we had plenty of customers so I could keep my job. I needed to be in that shop near to Kim. That was the easiest way."

"Where did you get the spell? Only it was pretty power-ful; even Margret, Shelley's mother didn't detect it."

"Jett acquired them. I don't know where from."

"Them? There was more than one?"

"I meant one. The love potion."

Lucy looked at me. Seth was clearly a terrible liar, and I felt he was owed for the shit he'd put us through, black-mailed or not. So I hit him with a powerful right hook, opening up a cut on his cheek.

"Okay, man. Okay. Not the face."

God he was vain.

He looked at Lucy. "There was a spell on that fortune

teller too. To block her visions. I distracted her in her shop and put something in her vodka. It lasts one to two weeks."

"Rav. Smack him for that." Lucy yelled. The demon she had brought with her backhanded him. It must have stung like a bitch.

"That felt wonderful, thank you for inviting me."

"Well, I can't do bad stuff now, so I needed an old colleague, and I thought of you."

"I'm honoured."

"Okay." I lifted my hand to quieten them all down. "Seth. You will be placed in a room here and put on constant guard until you can be released safely. We have your phone. Should you find some way to contact and warn Jett and endanger the pack then I will literally have you thrown to the wolves." Drool and growls came from the animals and the smell of urine filled the air as a wet patch seeped onto the chair. "Take him away and get him cleaned up please."

"So what now?" Lucy asked. "If you don't need me I'm going to collect Ebony from Theo's. She's been trialling the B&B, said it's been even better without the owners there, like a retreat. There's only been Mary around. I need to get Frankie on the case and then we'll get in touch with Theo and make sure Shelley has extra protection."

"When needed, I will send you two of my wolves to help protect Shelley and her baby."

"No, you'll need them all to fight Jett."

He shook his head.

"Like, my mate said on her note. I am expendable when it comes to the future ruler of Withernsea."

"You're both crazy, there's no wonder you get along." Lucy sighed and left taking her demon friend with her.

Left with the pack Edon asked for us to be excused for a moment and we stood to one end of the room.

"You are handling this beautifully, Darius. I would like to take this opportunity to propose you now take over from me as Alpha of the Withernsea pack."

I shook my head. "My father was scum."

"Yes he was, but you are not. So you have his blood running through your veins. I have been watching you, Darius. You command with ease and your wolf, he is growing ever stronger. You were born to be Alpha."

"I would not take your place. You have my utmost respect."

"I know. But to be honest I'm fancying a few holidays abroad. I'm not getting any younger."

"But what about Reid and Sonny? Do they not want to succeed you?"

"No. They don't have the slightest interest, and I believe it's because we weren't born to the position. You were. Meet Jett Alpha to Alpha on Thursday, Darius. We can have the coronation ceremony tomorrow evening."

I looked at Edon. Could I do this? Be Alpha? Lead the pack.

I imagined myself with Kim at my side. Yes, I could do this. For the pack, and for us. I would meet Jett on an equal footing. The ceremony would strengthen my wolf. It was time.

"Make the arrangements." I told Edon.

The ceremony took place the following evening. There was

a procedure to follow from the Handbook. Edon spoke first, retiring from his role and then he crowned me with a crown made of twigs and I said my own speech and commitment to my pack.

"I vow to protect you with my very last breath.

To my family.

WITHERNSEA."

Everyone raised a glass filled with either water or whiskey. "Alpha Darius. WITHERNSEA." My mum was crying, the rest of my family whooped and cheered. Then all changed into their animals and we ran through the woods and chased each other. My wolf was joyous, exultant. For the first time in my life I felt completely comfortable in my own skin and fur.

This is who I was born to be.

The Alpha.

CHAPTER Twenty-One

Lucy

I went to the farm to pick up Ebony.

She came to the door looking very relaxed. "Lucy? What are you doing here? They aren't here you know? Shelley has been turned."

"I know. I also know why you aren't having visions. Can I come in?"

"Course you can, love." Mary appeared in the doorway.

I walked inside and took a seat.

"So it would appear that a very clever spell was placed inside your vodka. Your visions won't return for up to two weeks, but then they should be back."

Ebony looked relieved.

"I thought you'd be devastated that they were coming back."

She shook her head, her eyes glassy. "I know they cause me a lot of upset, but they are my legacy, my life. Without them I feel I am nothing."

I placed a hand on her arm. "I understand." Before we set off, I filled her in on recent events. "Frankie is going to try to investigate who this wizard could be who is supplying Hogsthorpe with these potions. If he can find what was used to block your visions, he's hopeful that he could maybe work out a diluted potion that can give you some relief, and not wreck your liver."

"That would be ideal." Ebony said.

"Anyway, I've come to take you home. Now we know your visions will come back in time there's no reason for you to stay any longer, and I presume Theo and Shelley will want to be alone when she returns. We don't want her taking a chunk out of you."

"I suppose..." Ebony sighed. "All good things must come to an end, hey, Mary, my darling?"

"Yes, love. I will miss you, but Lucy's correct. Right now, I need to focus on getting things shipshape for my son and daughter-in-law's return."

"I will go pack my things." Ebony said and left the room.

The minute she was gone Mary let out a massive sigh of relief. "Thank God. I thought she'd never go. Bloody pampered princess wanting me to cater to her every whim. It's a B&B, not a five star hotel."

I laughed. "Mary. I'll leave you to get some rest. However," I stared at her. "If you are ever ready to leave and to go to heaven and to your husband just let me know. I'm sure I can arrange it for you. Help you."

"Oh wow. Gosh, I'd be reunited with Edward, but then I'd miss seeing my grandbaby..." Mary looked agitated.

"Mary, you don't have to make a decision now, and I don't know for definite that I could help you. I just have a feeling inside that I would be able to. I agree, for now your place is here, to care for Theo and Shelley and to meet that grandchild when she comes."

Mary nodded, but then stepped back a little, as if it had just dawned on her I worked for heaven. The place she was eventually destined for.

I dropped Ebony off home and then made my way home to Frankie. It was then I realised that Andrew hadn't been around... at all.

"Well, I'll not be too offended that it took you so long to notice my presence was missing." He appeared behind me with his arms folded.

"Sorry, things have been a bit hectic." I shrugged.

"Well, the reason I haven't been around is you no longer need me. My mission is accomplished and I've been given my job. I'm back as an earth angel, but I'm off to work in Hull, so you'll not be seeing me around."

"Why do I no longer need you? What did I do?"

"Without too many spoilers, Seth will return home to Hull, where I shall keep an eye on him. Also, despite your feelings for Kim with regard to her spending time with your fiance, you have put her needs above your own, and in doing so have done all you have the power to do in regards to keeping Shelley and the baby safe. In addition you just offered to help a ghost move to heaven if she wished. Your current jobs are done and Sophia is giving you a sabbatical for now as there is much change coming to Withernsea."

"Really? I have time off? I can help Frankie with his project."

"You can also arrange your wedding."

I beamed. "I can, can't I?" I flung my arms around Andrew causing his wings to pop out. "Ooops." I laughed. "Thank you, Andrew. I'm so glad you finally passed your angel exams."

"Me too." He said and then he disappeared leaving only a feather in his wake.

CHAPTER
Twenty-Two

Shelley

Dear God. I would never moan about period pains again. Literally I wouldn't either because now I was part-vampire I wouldn't have any more.

The first pains had come from the flu-like symptoms associated with me getting accustomed to my new blood type. Then my body had adjusted itself, becoming stronger. The baby had been kept on foetal monitoring throughout with no concerns at first until my stomach had swollen. Panic filled me and I screamed for my mum and for Theo, only to find on ultrasound that my turning had accelerated my pregnancy. I was now the equivalent of eight months pregnant on human terms.

I think my husband was close to a nervous breakdown.

"But we still should have months to prepare. The B&B isn't operational. We have no nursery done yet. What about childbirth classes? Names? We are completely unprepared."

Yeah. I'd just become part-vampire, and he was worrying about childbirth. Meanwhile, I'd spent two days resisting the urge to try to drain him of all his blood.

It was Thursday morning, and I was being discharged. Theo had gone home just before dawn to get the house ready. I had checked with him that he meant to ensure I had clean bedding and not to start painting the nursery.

And yes I was leaving in a morning. Being vampire mixed with wyvern and witch had produced a handy side-effect. I could still go out in daylight and we had found that I only needed a few hours sleep a day to reboot. I was super-charged. Food wise I required blood and a human diet in a mix. My cravings had subsided. It was just my strength I needed to get used to now.

Now on that side my husband couldn't wait, saying we'd be able to go for it all night long.

When the baby came he was going to have a huge shock.

"Okay. Have you got all your things?" Mum asked.

"Yes. Please take me home. I want my own bed and then after I'm rested I need to get caught up on the business and on anything else that's been happening in Withernsea."

While I'd been changing, everyone had left us alone. It had been strange, not being in the thick of Withernsea goings on.

"I wonder if Ebony has her visions back yet?"

"Well, let's get home and find out, shall we?"

Mum helped me pick up my belongings, and we left.

I let myself into the house, mum following behind me and was greeted with utter silence. No Mary, no Ebony. Nothing.

"Theo must have asked them to keep out of the way." I shrugged.

"Is there anything you need me to do while I'm here?" Mum asked.

"No. I'm just going to go straight to bed and set my alarm to get up with Theo, unless I wake earlier. I know I only need a minimum amount of sleep now, but my bed is warm, cosy, and has my husband in it."

"It's not cosy on his side, I'll bet."

"No, he's a tad on the cold side. Great in summer though." I'd remained the same temperature as before.

Mum kissed my cheek. "Right, you know where I am if you need me. I'll leave you to rest." She touched the bump. "Grandma's leaving, bye bump." My stomach lurched as the baby tried to move.

"It's getting tight in there now, isn't it bump?" I spoke to my belly, putting my hand on it.

Mum left and then I went to bed.

I managed to sleep until two in the afternoon. After lounging a little more, I got up, dressed and went down into the kitchen to get a drink of O-neg. Mary appeared through the doorway.

"I wondered where you were." I said to her.

"Your friend wore me out so I've been away resting."

"I know the feeling."

Mary's eyes went wide looking at my heavily pregnant stomach. "What has happened here? Is everything okay?"

"Everything's peachy. The turning brought my pregnancy on faster. I'm the equivalent of 8 months now. Where's Ebony?" I asked.

"Lucy came and took her home. She said Ebony's visions were down to a potion in her vodka and that they would come back within two weeks and Frankie would try to find the wizard who made the potion for Hogsthorpe and see if he could make a dilute version for her."

"Oh that's good news. I'd better put my phone on and see what else I've missed. Or I could just ring Kim that'd probably be quicker. She'll know everything." Then I paused. "Hang on, did you say potion for Hogsthorpe?"

"That's what Lucy said."

"On second thoughts I think I'll call Lucy first."

"I'll be making you a drink. Welcome home." Mary said and then she began busying herself with cups and bottles of blood.

"Shelley! How are you? Did everything go okay?"

"It went fine. Thanks for sorting Ebony out. What's this about some potion for Hogsthorpe?"

"Ah, okay. Are you sitting down, there's a lot to tell you."

"I wasn't but hold on." I plonked myself on the sofa. "Spill."

"So, let me say everything and then ask me questions or we'll be here all day."

"Lucy..."

"Fine. So Seth has been putting love potions in people's coffees to get them to return to the coffee shop to see him. Just so he can keep his job there and keep an eye on Kim. He's been blackmailed by Jett to do so. Jett also arranged for Seth to place a different potion in Ebony's vodka so that she wouldn't see his plans."

178

"And his plans are...?"

"To marry Kim and to take over the Withernsea pack."

"Huh, I bet Kim laughed him out of the building."

"They're getting married tomorrow evening."

"Whaaat?"

"He threatened to publicise your pregnancy and place a bounty on you and the baby. She put you first."

"Oh my God."

"Anyway, Darius did not accept this plan. So he's become Alpha of his pack and has a meeting with Jett tonight. It was basically a declaration of war and so this evening it is likely that either Jett or Darius may not survive."

"So what's the plan? What do we do?"

"The plan is that Darius and his pack go take down the Hogsthorpe pack."

I sat with my head in my hands. "And that's it? Does he not think Jett will no doubt have some spells or potions ready for this if he has a wizard in his pocket."

There was silence at the other end.

"We'd not thought of that."

"Well I'm thinking about it. What time is this meeting?"

"Nine pm."

"Right, I'll be there and so will Theo."

"No, Shelley. Kim would never forgive you, or me, if something happened to the baby."

"And I'd never forgive myself if something happened to Kim or Darius. Anyway when you see me, you'll realise trying to keep my pregnancy secret is no longer an option. Now, I'm going to call Darius, then my mother. We need to get our battle plans together. How's my best friend doing?"

"Not good. She's in the office and staring at the walls a lot. Apparently Jett has commanded that she move in with him. She spent last night in his room. He told her he wouldn't touch her until the mating but she still was made to share his bed. He's told her she will be there tonight at the meeting."

"In order to show Darius she belongs to Jett. He no doubt intends to parade her like a trophy."

"It would appear so."

"Yes, well it's about time Jett found out who rules things around here and it's not some jumped up mutt from Hogsthorpe."

"God, it's good to have you back, Shelley."

"Well, I'd like to say it's good to be back but once again someone is causing shit around the place. Time to clean up."

We said our goodbyes with an agreement that we would meet up with Darius later.

Now it was time to talk to the man himself and get our battle plans drawn up.

CHAPTER
Twenty-Three

Kim

It was time. We were sitting in the middle of one of the warehouses on the industrial estate. The room was vast. There were seats in a circle in the centre and Jett had a larger seat at the top of the room with a smaller one for me at his side. Like we were King and Queen.

Jett's mother had been on holiday and had returned this morning. She'd taken me to one side to let me know that although I would be an Alpha wife in name, she was the top woman of the pack and I would need to learn my place. She wasn't impressed therefore at having been relegated to one of the circle seats for the meeting.

The Hogsthorpe pack walked in, every one of them, around twenty in total. They took seats at the left-hand side of the circle. A tall man joined them. He was dressed in a suit. There was a knock on the door and Jett shouted "Enter."

In walked Darius and some of the Withernsea pack. I felt my heart might stop with shock.

But he didn't look at me. Not at all. His eyes were fixed on Jett's.

"Brother, so good to see you again." He said to Jett, and then he laughed. "I have brought some interested parties

181

with me." He turned to look at the suited man. "I note you have the same, so I presume you have no objections?"

"Not at all." Said Jett.

"Come." Commanded Darius.

In walked Lucy, Frankie, Theo, and Shelley. My eyes were almost out on stalks at seeing Shelley's pregnant belly. What the fuck? Had I been in a coma for a few months? Time travel? Had my dreams about flying around the world with David Tennant in the Tardis come true and then I'd been struck by a cruel form of amnesia?

I saw Jett's calm demeanor shake a little when he saw Shelley.

"Where is your Alpha, brother? We cannot start the meeting without your packs Alpha present."

"Oh, didn't you get the memo?" Darius smirked, taking a sheet of paper from his pocket and handing it to Jett. "I'm the Alpha of Withernsea now."

"You are?" I said loudly, forgetting myself.

"SILENCE." Jett roared.

Then all hell broke loose.

"DO NOT TELL MY MATE TO BE QUIET." Darius snarled.

"She is not your mate!"

I nodded at Darius behind Jett's back and mouthed. "I am."

One by one the pack turned into their wolves and then the suited man said an incantation and the Hogsthorpe wolves grew to twice their normal height and took on an eerie yellow glow.

Shelley rose. "Jett Conall. I command that you refrain from this course of action."

Jett looked at her. "Which would be great if we were on

Withernsea turf, but we aren't. We're in Hogsthorpe, and you don't rule here."

Shelley looked shocked. The suited man smirked.

The wolves got up until one wolf flanked every one of the other pack and each of my friends. I had a wolf from both packs appear either side of me and Jett stalked over to Darius.

We had no chance. I knew Shelley was a powerful witch and I could see her calculating moves, but how could she possibly do anything without the loss of life here? I just didn't see a way out.

There was a stalemate, and I knew that as they had made the protest it was down to Darius and his pack to make the first move, or withdraw and give in.

I watched as Darius bowed his head.

I wanted to cry. I wanted to yell for him to fight for me, but I knew to do so would be to put his pack and my friends at risk and I couldn't do that. But there was one thing I could do.

"Whether you win against Darius or not, I will not marry you. You might be the leader of Hogsthorpe but you are not the boss of me."

"Or me." A familiar voice came from the ceiling. As she dropped she changed into wolf form and she landed directly on Jett's body. He had the room surrounded, but he'd not had the ceiling watched, and Alyssa had decided to join the party. I'd never seen a wolf like it. She was lithe, her muscles rippled, and her teeth when she roared were pincer sharp. Jett swung out with a claw knocking her to the floor and Darius roared moving to his sister's side. I looked over at Shelley who smiled at me as her eyes turned blue. Then she lifted her hands and her blue webs wrapped around the suited man. He'd been so distracted by Alyssa, he'd dropped his guard. The minute Shelley wrapped him in her webs, the spell on the Hogsthorpe pack broke and they returned to their normal size. But where I expected Hogsthorpe to launch into an attack on Withernsea for attacking their Alpha they stood still, and watched as Alyssa leaped back up from the ground and bit down on Jett's neck, tearing at his jugular. Blood spurted across the room and Jett's body slumped across the floor, remaining in wolf form. Red blood pooled around his black fur.

His mother let out a howl of anguish and then leapt for Alyssa, but she was no match either and succumbed to the same fate as her son.

There was silence and then Alyssa returned back into her human form. Blood dripped from her mouth.

One by one the wolves also returned to their human forms. Whoa. That was a whole lot of naked.

"And the lesson is don't threaten the family of a female wolf with pre-menstrual tension." Alyssa spat.

"How the hell did you do that?" I asked.

Darius turned to me. "It would appear that while I thought my sister had been up to no good with teenage boys, she'd actually been training in an aerial circus appearing in town. She's been making pocket money appearing at 8pm every night."

He shook his head. "Sisters."

"Just got your ass out of trouble." She said, and then she turned to the other pack. "What's going on anyway? Why didn't you fight?"

One of the men, an older one, stepped forward. "Our Alpha had become dangerous of late. Unpredictable. And it is not of our ways to war using magic. It is against the rules of the shifter handbook."

Darius spoke, though to be honest I was having trouble

keeping my eyes on his mouth.

"You can elect a new leader now, or you can pledge allegiance and join Withernsea. It is up to you."

"May we have a few moments?"

"Of course."

They went over to one corner of the warehouse. I ran to Darius. He flung me around in his arms and I wrapped my legs around his waist. We kissed each other over and over. Then he put me down.

"What happens now? With Jett and his mother, I mean?"

"The Hogsthorpe pack shall bury their bodies somewhere undetectable."

"He would have killed you, wouldn't he?" I said.

"Yes. We are not like humans. In animal form sometimes we have to fight to the death. Jett would have had us all slaughtered."

I nodded as I knew he spoke the truth.

"I must go to see Shelley."

"And I need to talk to Alyssa and speak to the pack."

I walked away and went up to my best friend. Frankie was currently sat next to Mr Suited and Booted.

"So, who's the dude?" I asked her.

"He's shy and doesn't want to give his name. He's being taken to the Caves where he'll be imprisoned until he wants to speak. I've disabled his powers, so he's no threat to anyone."

"How come you didn't detect the potions though? Does that mean his powers were stronger?"

"No. I believe mine were weaker. My pregnancy was taking it out of me, making my human body weaker. My wyvern and witch side were supporting my humanity and therefore weren't operating at one hundred percent efficiency. Now I've been turned and have no human part, I'm stronger than ever. And my mum was distracted that day. I was having a good old whine about life."

"You appear to be ready to give birth. I'm guessing that's due to the vamp mojo?"

"Indeed." Theo joined us. "And has thus given me quite the dilemma. It would appear the B&B shall be delayed once more as now all my attention needs to be given to the nursery and to organise things for our daughter seeing as she'll be making an appearance a lot sooner than we thought."

"Hey, what's happening?" Shelley looked over my shoulder.

The Hogsthorpe pack one by one stood in front of Darius, went to their knees, dipped their heads and murmured something. We moved closer to hear the words.

"I pledge my allegiance to the Withernsea pack and to you Alpha Darius..."

"I pledge..."

Every wolf there did the same and then Darius spoke to all of the assembled wolves.

"I thank you for your pledges. After speaking to my younger brother just now I would like to note our future plans. I will happily rule you all until such time as my sister, Alyssa, becomes eighteen years of age. At which time, in the interests of modern times and with my pride at her courageous actions today, I shall offer the Alpha position to her. The first time a woman will have been offered the post."

A joyous roar came from the rest of the pack which surprised me given how a lot of men still thought women belonged in the kitchen. Then again she did still have blood stains around her mouth and had killed an Alpha and his mother like swatting pesky flies, so I guess they might just be shit scared of arguing the point.

Alyssa's mouth dropped open. "Thanks, bro, but I'm planning on going away with the circus. No one else has an aerial artist who turns into a wolf by 'magic'."

"Please tell me you have not been revealing yourself."

"Calm down. I shall behave, but only until I'm eighteen and then you'll just have to put up with it."

"Not as Alpha, I won't."

"As a *brother*, you will."

"Okay, okay." I said stepping between them. "If all business is concluded then can we get out of here? I'd quite like to go home now."

"Could you kindly get us some robes, or spare clothes." Darius asked one of the ex-Hogsthorpe shifters.

Once dressed he took my hand. "Come on, I'll take you back to your place."

I stared at him. "I said I wanted to go home, Darius."

His forehead bunched in confusion.

"To my future pack. To my future family. I belong with you, Darius, and I don't want to waste another minute."

CHAPTER Twenty-Four

Kim

I looked at the quickly printed invitations. With the short notice I think I'd done an excellent job.

You are invited to the wedding of:

Kimberly Louise Fletcher and Darius Wild

Friday 9 February 2018
10pm
The Main Hall
Withernsea Caravan Park

A celebration party will take place straight after the ceremony.

Please be aware that guests at the wedding MAY see naked bodies during the celebrations due to wolf/human transition

It's so good when your boutique owning friend has contacts. She managed to get me the most beautiful dress. It wasn't a full proper wedding dress. A sleek dress with white lacy sleeves, it came to just below my knee and looked elegant. She curled my hair into ringlets and did my make-up.

I looked in the mirror. I looked happy. Something I'd not seen in my reflection in quite a while.

"Thank you, Ebony." I said.

"I told you so. Told you, you were meant for him."

"Yes, alright, Mrs Clever Clogs. You were right. There I said it. Are you happy now?"

"Yes darling, I just needed to hear you say the words."

Shelley was walking around whining. "Look at me. I'm a walking marquee." She'd had to be changed into a larger dress due to her ever-expanding stomach.

"Excuse me. Today is all about me." I reminded her.

She burst into a peal of laughter and clutched her tummy. "Oh it is good to have my best friend back."

Freya stood in the doorway. "He's here. It's time to go."

I turned to her and smiled. My own mum wasn't here, but I didn't need her. I had Freya now.

Frankie walked me down the aisle taking the place of my father. I'd thought about who could accompany me and had decided that Frankie was kind of my male best friend. He'd been honoured, and Lucy had looked really happy when she'd found out, although for some reason she thought I'd asked him ages ago.

And then I was at the front and everyone else faded from my attention. It was just me and Darius.

The registrar spoke. Before I knew it he said the words I'd been waiting for.

"I now declare you Alpha and wife."

And the celebrations began.

At midnight, Darius and I walked down to the yurt together. The whole inner woodland had been decorated in fairy lights.

"Finally, I've got you alone." Darius said, his voice low and husky. Last night his mum had insisted we sleep in separate beds and that he didn't see me today as it was bad luck. You'd think she'd have let tradition ride after we'd all just survived a pack war but no.

"You have." I looked up at him. His eyes flashed his wolf look for a moment. Desire pooled low in my belly.

"Wife. I have needs and I command you come into this yurt and attend to them."

I bellowed with laughter. "If you're going to start talking to me like that, we'll be divorced before sunrise."

"Never." He growled. "You're my mate for life."

With that he picked me up and carried me through the yurt's opening and put me on my feet next to the bed. He turned me so that my back was to him and he unzipped my dress. I let it shimmy to my feet and he picked it up and placed it over the back of a chair. I was now standing in front of him in my bridal undies. White, lacy, and oh... already off.

He in fact had peeled my thong off with his teeth, eliciting shivers down my spine. Goose bumps rose on my arms. He stood behind me, his erection against my ass and he cupped my breast in his hand.

"All mine." He said.

I turned around in his arms and cupped his pec.

"All mine." I repeated.

He threw me on the bed. "You leave me no choice but to shag this insolence out of you."

"Ooh if you insist." I replied, and then I couldn't speak any more because his mouth was on mine.

He trailed his mouth down the side of my neck and all the way down to my thighs and then he nestled between them and his mouth fastened on my core.

"Oh my God." I screamed as his tongue flicked over my nub and inside me. He drove me wild which was ironic given that was now my last name. I was Mrs Kimberly Wild. Oh. My. God. My name was Kim Wild—with the exception of a missing 'e' on my surname, I now sounded like a 1980's pop star. I felt like bursting into a chorus of 'You came' but given we were having sex right now I felt it might be a tad Freudian.

I exploded on his mouth. While I got my breath back, Darius moved up and over my body. "Babe, I saw stars. It was that good." I told him. He shook his head at me. "Kim, you can see stars. There's a space in the yurt roof, where the smoke from the fire exits."

"Oh yeah."

"But maybe I caused some extra ones." He said, lining himself up at my entrance.

"Are you ready to properly become my mate?" He asked.

"Yes." I nodded, "now get inside me already."

He pushed deep, and I moaned in lust. He took his time building us up to our climaxes and then just as I started to lose it I felt the graze of sharpened teeth and he bit my neck.

"Oooooohhhhh."

We both came hard and then I felt a fizzing sensation throughout my body. I saw Darius change into his wolf before my eyesight went blurry and then a weird rippling sensation took over. It wasn't painful, it was just very, very, strange.

My eyesight cleared, and I stared at my arm. It had fur, and I had claws. I was a fucking wolf! My fur was dark brown. Was there a mirror here? Oh, yes, in the corner of the yurt. I padded over to it.

God, I even looked good as a wolf.

Yes, you do. My husband's voice echoed in my mind.

You can read my thoughts?

Yes, and you can read mine. You can control it, but yes we can communicate in this way as pack.

HMMMM, can you read this thought?

The wolf bounded over and confirmed he could indeed.

After we'd made love in our wolf forms, we ran through the woods together. It was an amazing experience, so freeing. I didn't realise however that I'd run right up to the Hall entrance where some guests including Frankie, Lucy, Shelley, and Theo, still stood. In my surprise I lost my wolf fur.

Yes, the bride stood in front of her guests in her birthday suit.

Lucy dived to cover Frankie's eyes. "What are you doing, woman? It's nothing I haven't seen before."

"Yes, I'm well aware of the fact she's your ex."

"I meant as a physician you daft bat."

Theo took off his suit jacket and walked over to me. "Here you go, Mrs Wild. We don't want you catching a chill."

Meanwhile my best friend stood there laughing. Pointing... and laughing.

"Oh my God, I laughed so much I weed myself." She giggled.

"Not wee, bestie." I told her. "Not wee."

Suddenly she wasn't laughing anymore.

Theo started shouting. "We need an ambulance. My

wife's having a baby. Help please." I left them to it as my mother-in-law took over.

I walked over to Frankie. "I have you covered. Walk into the centre of the woods, then yurt number one is free if you want it. It's just been readied for guests. I'll ask them to relaunder afterwards."

"Thank you. I need to do something, she's looking murderous."

Frankie spoke to Lucy and rolling her eyes at him she set off into the woods mumbling that he 'would owe her big time for looking for rare insects'."

"What are you up to Mrs Wild?"

"Come to the woods with me and see."

"We just got back from there."

"So?"

He followed me having been told to be extremely quiet. We watched from a distance as Frankie got down on bended knee in the woodland, surrounded by fairy lights. And then dozens upon dozens of white feathers fell from nowhere and covered the floor in a blanket of softness. It was beautiful.

Lucy nodded and said "yes," and he placed a ring on her finger.

I'd offered the yurt, but they clung to each other, kissed, and then walked back towards the party. I would bet they were going home.

"Well, it's just you and me again, and a yurt. What shall we do, hubby?" I asked.

Then a voice shouted out behind me.

"They're back. Kim, the voices are back."

I sighed. "Ebony, that's great, and all, but you didn't need to rush to tell me."

"But you were in my vision..."

Oh no. What had she seen now? Was I about to cause an apocalypse?

Darius looked worried. "What did you see Ebony?"

"I saw a wedding dress. I was wearing it, and I was standing in a Church. Kim was my bridesmaid."

"I thought you weren't supposed to see your own future?" I queried.

"That's just it, Kim. I could see I was getting married but I couldn't see the groom! I don't even have a boyfriend, so who the hell am I marrying?" She screamed.

"Well, I don't know, but I do know who I just married, Chica, so you go get a vodka and I'll go get my man." I winked. "We'll sort it, Ebs."

Then I dragged my husband back into our yurt. It was time to get... WILD.

THE END

So, who is Ebony's mystery groom?
Find out in H**ere for the Seer**
Coming July 2018
Pre-order here

FREE BOOK

Get your FREE book

RECEIVE YOUR FREE E-COPY OF THE
SUPERNATURAL DATING AGENCY PREQUEL

DATING SUCKS

When you subscribe to my weekly newsletter.

Yes, that's right. This short story prequel will be sent to you
FREE when you subscribe.

Before the vampire wanted a wife, he went to a speed dating night...

Shelley Linley attends a speed dating event, leaving with a
potential date, and a new best friend, while avoiding the
cold-handed weirdo who fell on the floor clutching his ears.

After dating disasters and meeting a strange woman who

says she can see the future, Shelley decides to set up her own dating agency for Withernsea's singles.

Can she find love for others even though she can't find it for herself? Her love life sucks, and she's yet to find out that's been her destiny all along...

My weekly newsletter sent Mondays contains my book news, exclusive content, and sales and new release information.

Sign up here

ABOUT Andie

Andie M. Long is author of the popular Supernatural Dating Agency series amongst many other books.

She lives in Sheffield with her son and long-suffering partner.

When not being partner, mother, writer, or book editor, she can usually be found on Facebook or walking her whippet, Bella.

www.andiemlongwriter.com

 twitter.com/andiemichelle

instagram.com/andiemlongwriter

BB bookbub.com/authors/andie-m-long

SUPERNATURAL DATING AGENCY

The Vampire wants a Wife

A Devil of a Date

Hate, Date, or Mate

THE ALPHA SERIES

The Alphabet Game

The Alphabet Wedding

The Calendar Game

The Baby Game

The Alpha Series Boxset

The Alphabet Game: Play It Playbook

THE BALL GAMES SERIES

Balls (Book One)

Snow Balls (Book Two)

New Balls Please (Book Three)

Balls Fore (Book Four)

Jingle Balls (Book Five)

Curve Balls (Book Six)

Birthing Balls (Book Seven)

The Ball Games Bundle (One to Four)

STANDALONE TITLES

UNDERNEATH

JOURNEY TO THE CENTRE OF MYSELF

SAVIOUR

MINE

THE BUNK UP
(co-written with DH Sidebottom)

Receive **DATING SUCKS** ebook for FREE by signing up to Andie's newsletter here

Made in the USA
San Bernardino, CA
10 April 2019